WHEN IT COMES TO REVENGE - TIMING IS EVERYTHING.

GORDON
BROWN

59 MINUTES

"Great stuff - '59 Minutes' is a pacy, intriguing crime thriller with a stunning conclusion."

Helen Fitzgerald

Also by Gordon Brown

Falling

Published by Fledgling Press 2009

"Falling is an accomplished rapid fire debut thriller with a cast of dark characters guaranteed to keep you turning the pages until the very last twist."
Richard Draycott, Editor – The Drum

"Brown keeps a firm, skilful grip on his material in what turns out to be a very promising debut novel."
The Herald

"With its sharp, witty dialogue, plot twists and no small dose of humour, this debut novel kept me thoroughly entertained."
Alison Lawrence

" Chaos reigns as the plot comes thick and fast in this thriller told from alternating perspectives of a brilliantly drawn cast of characters. If Guy Ritchie is looking for his next crime caper, he could do worse."
Daily Record

59 MINUTES

Gordon Brown

Fledgling Press 2010

First Published in 2010 by Fledgling Press
7 Lennox Street, Edinburgh, EH4 1QB, Scotland
www.fledglingpress.co.uk

All the characters in this book are imaginary. Any resemblance to real people, living or dead, is purely coincidental. Some places are real, others are in the imagination of the author. Any errors are those of the author.

A CIP catalogue reference for this book is available from the British Library

ISBN: 978 1 905916 25 2

Cover by overflowartworkanddesign.co.uk
Printed and Bound by Thomson Litho Ltd,
East Kilbride, Scotland

About the author

Gordon Brown was born and lives in Glasgow. He is married with two children - having spent twenty five years in the sales and marketing world working on everything from alcohol to global charities and from TV to lingerie.

Gordon started out life packing shelves for Sainsbury's before moving to Canada to join the brewery business. He set up his own marketing business in 2001 and has an honours degree from Strathclyde along with an MBA from Nottingham Trent University.

Gordon has been writing for pleasure for some twenty years and this is his second novel following the success of his debut - Falling.

This book is dedicated to my mum - thanks for everything.

Prologue

The bastard kissed the tips of his fingers, reached down and patted me on the head. I looked up and saw the smile leave his face.

'So different. It should have all been so different.'

I struggled to get up but my attacker and the man from the Spanish photo were good for the game and I was pinned to the floor. The first fist caught me behind the ear - the knuckleduster slicing open my skull. Snap, crackle and pop and the second fist mashed my nose to mince.

Just the beginning. I tried to curl into a ball. Just the beginning.

The door to the room closed as the bastard left and it was time for more pain. The attacker reached between my legs and grabbed at my balls. The squeeze was so hard it felt like one of them burst. A thumb searched for my left eye socket and a forefinger for my right - fluid spurted and darkness fell.

Then they got serious.

Chapter 1

The clock on the wall says eleven oh one. The second hand has crested the apex and we are now into the second minute after the hour and counting. I can't see it move but, with a fascination that owes everything to my circumstances, I know the tick of that second hand intimately, lovingly, fearfully and a shed load of other adverbs that would bore you to the core.

Fifty eight minutes and fifty four seconds to go. Not long now. There are important things that I need to tell you in the minutes that remain to me. So many things, that we may not have the time we need.

But I will try.

Why? Why will I try to tell you these things? Because I need to tell someone and you are better placed than most, far better placed than most, to listen and understand. Listening is not even your responsibility. Understanding is what you need to do. It is up to me to make you listen. If I fail, you will drift away like the sober leaving the drunk.

But I doubt this.

As we travel together down this short path, there will be a number of questions that you will want to ask. I'll tell you now that I won't answer them. I'm sorry I can't be more co-operative but debate is a locked five bar gate on our trip.

Can you also forgive me if I become a little vague or distracted? My mind may wander. It is inevitable. It is probably essential. My story may need some detours to make sense.

To help, I have left a diary, of sorts, for you to read. It is there beside you. The big black book with the gold block lettering on the spine. Who gave me it is of no great importance. It is nothing more than the sort of gift you would get from a distant aunt at Christmas.

Please do not pick it up. Not now.

So, where should I start? Where would you start with a clock ticking like a time bomb?

'Start at the beginning and go on. And when you reach the end stop.'

It is a bad lift from Alice in Wonderland but you get the gist.

By the way it is nearly eleven oh two. I must move on.

Chapter 2

I was born in the west end of Glasgow. Partick to be exact. I was never the healthiest of kids. I had a tendency to monopolise whatever bug was doing the rounds. I missed much of my schooling, replacing it with an in-depth knowledge of doctor's surgeries, hospitals, my bedroom, my grandmother's bedroom and a private TB clinic. Suffice to say I left school with no qualifications and little prospects.

It would be nice to say I went on to make good and earn my fortune the honest way. An entrepreneur of note. But that would be a crock of crap. True, I made money but I also managed to make a turkey sandwich of my life on the way. I held promise and I excelled in places that others failed but ultimately I washed my life down a large plug hole and watched the water spin away - carrying my heart beats and my ambition to a dark place.

After leaving school, I found employment with a friend of my father. It was menial work. The sort that requires little thought, a lot of graft and rewards you with a thin pay packet.

My father's friend was a man called George Matthews. George owned an engineering firm on the outskirts of Glasgow that employed twenty men who slaved hard to produce spare parts for the automotive industry. The hours were long and the factory had to sweat for its money. Saturday and even Sunday shifts were the norm for the first two years of my working life. I lost contact with my schoolmates and found it hard to acquire new friends at work.

Being far younger than anyone else in the building my nickname was not very original - 'Junior' - and since the work's recreation revolved around the Lame Duck pub I was, at sixteen years of age, excluded from that particular avenue of respite.

Michael Tolt was my only friend of note from back then. It is Michael, dead these many years, that is, in part, responsible for me sitting here talking to you.

When I joined the firm I was his saviour. In an instant, the scorn that the factory poured upon its youngest member fell from his shoulders and onto mine. I think he always knew this was a shit deal and in compensation he became the one person I could talk to at break time or see outside of work.

He was a fanatic for football, and for Partick Thistle in particular. Over the years he dragged me along to a nightmare collection of games. He never tired of his obsession and was rewarded for his long term service with the club when, on the 23rd October 1971, against all predictions, they took on the might of Celtic in the League Cup final and hammered them four – one.

I still remember standing on the terraces at Hampden Park at half time - Partick were four up against one of the best sides in Europe. To say that there was a party atmosphere wasn't even close to the truth on that day. There may never be a finer moment to be a Jags fan.

But I had no love of the club and I was the least

excited person in the Partick Thistle throng. But the game did bring one defining moment with it. After the match I was permitted entry into the hallowed halls of The Lame Duck for my first drink. Having turned eighteen the day before, the stained floorboards, dank smoky air and rank smell of a million men's farts were mine for the taking.

Eleven oh four and ten seconds. Time slips past so fast. I must keep my foot on the gas.

I left Matthews Engineering two months later. I couldn't take it anymore. The combination of poor hours, the lack of pay and the endless insults forced me out and onto the 'Bru' - to survive on state handouts.

Neither my mother nor my father were in the happy world about this. They were reliant on my contribution to the house to help offset the mountain of debt they had acquired. No, and let's be honest about this, the debt was not theirs but my father's, and my father's alone, the local bookie being the open drain he so easily poured our cash into.

When I left the job I intended to find other employment as quickly as possible. But Britain was heading for its worst recession since the thirties and with no qualifications, no skills and, probably most damning of all, no connections I was prime meat for the local criminal fraternity. After six months of fruitless interviews and rejections Michael Tolt stepped in with an offer that was hard to refuse.

He informed me, over a pint in The Lame Duck, that a friend of his was looking for a reliable lad to run some errands. This friend needed someone who could keep his mouth shut, do as he was told and, in return, would receive five pounds a week. The icing was that I could still sign on.

A week later I met Tony 'the Nose' Campbell.

Chapter 3

'the Nose' lived in one of the better houses in the West End of Glasgow: a home stuffed with antiques that meant nothing to me but were expensive as hell. My interview with him was short and sweet. I was told that the job was mine as long as my lips didn't part and I took orders like an SS guard. I agreed and was dispatched to the east end of the city with a list of addresses scribbled on the back of a fag packet.

In each case I was expected to turn up at the door and inform the inhabitant that 'the Nose' had sent me. In return I was usually given an envelope, which I stuffed in my pocket.

The door openings were never pleasant. I was never welcome. I was never asked in. I was verbally and, occasionally, physically abused. But most people still handed over their envelope.

On the rare occasions I was given no envelope, I had instructions to circle their names with a red pen. When I handed the envelopes, and the list, back to 'the Nose', he would ask if anyone had 'Red Ringed' him today. If I said 'yes', a strange smile would cross his lips.

A 'Red Ringed' house always had an envelope waiting for me on my next visit - the reluctant giver with a face that looked like it had met with a train head on.

Occasionally a house would be struck off my list. Usually a multiple 'Red Ringer'.

I once stumbled on a funeral leaving a 'Red Ringer' and I made the mistake of asking who had died. The woman spat in my face.

I was no fool. I knew what was going on. Within the first week of my new job I was more than aware I was collecting money for a loan shark. The abuse I received left me in no doubt. But 'the Nose' would simply tell me to grin and bear it and point out that I was really doing them a service, providing a source of cash when people were most in need. In his mind it was his way of serving the community. I adopted the same attitude and put my head down and worked hard.

Six months into my new life 'the Nose' asked if I would like to up my wages. Do cats lick their balls was my reply and so I was introduced to Sammy Dall.

Sammy was a small weedy man who never looked you in the eye. He was given the job of instructing me in the finer details of acquiring new clients - for which I would receive a percentage of the profits.

It was a reflection on the state of the economy that I earned ten pounds within two days of starting my new role. It was easy money. Sammy was a great teacher, and a past master at drawing in punters and fleecing them. After a couple of weeks I was given a pitch near some local shops and business boomed.

Did I feel remorse at what I did? Not really. Most of the people were only into 'the Nose' for small amounts and, although the interest rate was crippling, it was survivable.

By then I was no longer collecting door to door. People came to me to pay up and if they didn't I simply added them to the 'Red Ring' list, and someone else sorted it out.

The down side was that it was a cold job in winter. There were days when I would have loved to use the local café as a meeting place but my clients didn't want others to know their business. So I stood in the cold behind the City Bakeries, breathing in the smell of baking bread while my feet froze solid.

I had been three years with 'the Nose' when I was first lifted by the police. Things were motoring along nicely. I would never be rich but, having acquired a car and, better still a license - obtained with the help of a two hundred quid bribe to a bent driving examiner, I was now mobile and I was a lot better off than most on my street.

My incarceration was a direct result of my love for beer. The Lame Duck had opened my eyes to the wonders of McEwan's Export and then to the joys of Grant's whisky. After that there was no looking back. I took to them both like an alcoholic duck to a pond full of ethanol.

With my wallet never short of a five pound note, I could indulge my liking for alcohol in a manner that my mates could only achieve through the cheap stuff from the off license or the dreaded home made hooch that some of their fathers made.

It was a wet Tuesday evening when the police felt my collar. Life seemed full of wet Tuesday evenings. It's a Glasgow thing. Rain and Tuesdays. I had been in the Lame Duck. Why not? It was far warmer than my mother's flat? Central heating was still a wonder of the future to my family, and the pub came with the built in warmth of humanity.

I was six sheets to the wind and should have been in a good mood. But I was in a shit mood. I'm not a violent drunk but on that night I had been in a boilermaker of an argument with Michael who, smashed out of his face, had accused me of being gay. To cap it he had done so in front of the regular church going assembled congregation of the Lame Duck by calling me a poof. Political correctness, like central heating, was also a thing of the future.

To be fair to Michael the evidence was quite damning in his eyes. I'd had no girlfriend since school. And even then it had been little more than a peck on the cheek from Mandy McCulloch. I openly shunned the frequent stag nights if strippers were involved and a recent attempt to set me up with Michael's youngest sister had been a disaster - I had ended the evening by calling her a frigid, ugly cow. To add cream to the cake I had done this in front of Michael.

Despite, in my opinion, my description of his sibling being perfectly accurate, Michael had challenged my sexuality, subjected me to a verbal battering in the extreme and I had stormed out of the pub looking for something to hit.

Unfortunately, on that particular cold wet Tuesday night, I chose to hit an off duty policeman, who, with great aplomb and very little effort, arm locked me and marched me to the local police station. Appearing at the sheriff court the next morning, I was fined twenty pounds and bound over to keep the peace.

I kept all this from my mum. She needed more

grief like a hole in her skull. My father's heart had given out on the Christmas Eve of 1972 and my mother was terminally ill with cancer.

I spent most nights back then either drunk as a skunk in the Lame Duck or up at the hospital. By the time I was arrested my mother's life revolved around the diamorphine they were feeding into her drip. The money from the loan sharking had gone to providing the best care that could be bought back then. It still wasn't much but it was better than nothing. At least she spent her last few days in the comfort of a private room.

My altercation with the local constabulary did not go down well with 'the Nose'. Despite my best efforts, word of my arrest got back to him and he was pissed off. He liked his workers to keep a clean slate. The less interest we generated from the authorities the better. I was now tarnished and 'the Nose' was angry, but he wasn't stupid. I was good at my job. As such I was kept on but my wages were cut and, when I tried to protest I lost a tooth and gained six stitches for my efforts.

Eleven eight and six seconds.

Chapter 4

On the day my mum died I was freezing my knackers off behind the City Bakeries. 'the Nose' found out at ten in the morning but didn't send anyone to tell me until after three - hence ensuring that I had collected the day's takings.

The funeral was small and depressing. I paid for the best of coffins and a do at the Partick Halls. There were twelve of us in a space built for hundreds. The following day I handed back the keys to the hovel that had been my home since birth and, with the help of 'the Nose', obtained a deposit on a small flat off Hyndland Rd in Glasgow's west end.

I had stepped on to the property ladder.

Six months later 'the Nose' joined my mother in Maryhill cemetery.

He died in a fire.

As I stood outside the shell of his house a policeman, with the hint of a smile, told me that 'the Nose' was no more. What the policeman didn't tell me was that 'the Nose' had, prior to being burnt alive, been divested of both hands, his genitals and a large proportion of his face.

'the Nose' had been in debt to people far uglier than himself for more cash than he could ever pay back. There's irony in there somewhere.

'the Nose' had met his match and I was out of a job.

The next few months were hard. As soon as word got round that 'the Nose' was history a range of suitors came to call on my customers. I was on my own and my competition came with a heavy mob attached. I tried to keep some of the customers but in the end I lost them all. The new boys on the block simply wiped a percentage of 'the Nose's' slate clean and they were suddenly heroes. I was booted off my patch and fell back on what little savings I had.

In the scheme of things my next move could have been smarter but I was badly missing spare change in my pocket and, when Michael gave me the name of another contact I went along for the ride.

This time it wasn't loan sharking. It was lower than that.

I was a look out.

My first job was keeping watch for a local gang on the back lot of an old disused bus station. I was there to ensure that the gang could carry out their various escapades without fear of being caught. It was down to me to give them the few vital seconds to make good an escape when the law, or other interested bodies made an unexpected appearance.

For my pains I would catch a pay packet of three quid for the job. I moved into 'look out' land and, on a good week, I could pull in six jobs. It kept me in beer and fags.

It was then that I discovered I had more than a small gift for breaking and entering. It wasn't something I had ever tried but it was something that I would excel at.

I stumbled upon my talent when Jimmy Call, the leader of my new gang, turned his attention to the local betting shop and the safe that squatted in the premise's back room.

Rumours had abounded for years about the amount of money that lay in that little grey treasure trove. The fact that it had sat untouched for more than ten years was down to the evil bastard who owned the bookies - one Malcolm Smillie, a man of little compassion.

Jimmy hatched a plan to do over the shop and make off with the safe. It was a crazy plan from the start. At its best it would seriously hack off Malcolm and at worst we would all end up in the canal wearing the latest in heavyweight body bags. But Jimmy was short on the smarts, cased the joint for over a week and announced that the back door was the weak point - everyone knew weak points were not the issue but this passed him by.

On the day of the job, Andy Hall, the gang's break-in wizard, was caught stealing a car and was out of the equation. Jimmy decided to go in anyway and I was roped in to help cart the safe away while Jimmy's wee brother, John, took on the look out duties.

I stood back and watched as Jimmy tried to use the lock pick that Andy had given him. Getting nowhere quick he changed tack and took an axe to the door but, after half an hour, the back door showed no signs of budging. Metal doors are pretty effective barriers to entry.

In frustration Jimmy threw the lock pick away and for reasons that were pure serendipity, I picked it up and asked if I could have a go. The gang laughed but Jimmy said he didn't care so I tried my hand.

To tell you it felt right from moment one is an understatement. It felt great. As soon as I poked the wire into the key hole I knew I was on a fresh road. It just felt perfect. Like an extension to my hand.

I twisted and turned and the clicks of the levers being worked were Mozart playing in my ears. I hadn't a Scooby what I was doing but after a few seconds the lock popped open. Jimmy swore for ten seconds before pushing past me and into the back shop.

It would have been nice if my first job had been a success but it wasn't to be. True, the safe existed but it was bolted securely to the concrete floor and would have taken ten men ten days with a pick axe each to even worry it. On top of this there was a sign, taped to the front of the safe, which read:

'Jimmy. If you are reading this, I'd think about taking a holiday – permanently.'

We all ran and three days later we heard that Jimmy was in the Southern General with an assortment of broken bones.

Shit happens like an evil dose of the runs when you play with the big boys.

Chapter 5

My new found skill was soon in demand. I foolishly bragged about it and I was picked up by Martin Sketchmore, a rare anglophile in our midst, an old acquaintance of Michael Tolt and, to top it all, a fellow Partick Thistle nutter – go figure.

'Been hearing that you are good with locks.'

His accent was thick with somewhere in England, but not thick enough for me to place it. I nodded.

'Got a job for you.'

It was a doddle. A little house breaking. The home of a Mrs McCafferty as it turned out. Top floor flat in Meadowpark Street in the east end of the city. Easy pickings. She was at the bingo and Martin had his eyes on her husband's paypacket.

'She keeps it behind the clock. Friday night, the old man brings it in, takes out his beer money and the rest is for her. Today was bonus time at Mellowes.'

Mellowes was a small engineering works that Martin skivvied in and Mr McCafferty gaffered for. Hence his intimate knowledge of all things mantle-piece in the McCafferty household.

Martin had planned to go in earlier in the evening but a few pints got in the way and, later that Friday we could be found climbing the stairs to the McCaffertys' home - ears alive for any sounds.

At the top of the last flight I was faced with a storm door. It was locked but a few seconds with a piece of wire and a nail file and it was open.

The inner door was all glass - swanky as hell for those days. Martin pushed me to one side and booted the glass. Shards showered around us and before they could settle Martin was in and out, pay packet stuffed in his pocket. The McCaffertys didn't make it out of the bedroom before we were gone.

It hadn't occurred to me that they might be in.

I got a tenner for that job – Mrs McCafferty's old man must have got a hell of a bonus for Martin to pay me a tenner.

And so it went on. I was a gun for hire. You want in. I get you there. But mostly I worked with Martin. It was a hell of a time. I wish I could tell you more. I really do but the clock is ticking.

I was on the up again but on a downward track – if that makes any sense. I was rising up the criminal world but sliding down the social scale on the polite side of society.

After a year of lock picking with Martin I wanted to go freelance. I fancied the lion's share of the profits from a job - after all Martin would have fuck all if it wasn't for me. I'm sure you know what I mean? So I bided my time, waiting for the right job.

It arrived in the late summer of 1976.

We were working the south side of Glasgow as the west and east were getting a little too hot. The police were on to us and word was on the street that there was some money in it for anyone that could turn us in. Forget CSI - it didn't exist back then - grassing up was far more effective and some of my fellow thieves would be happy to drop me in it.

Especially those who kept their freedom by dropping the odd word in the police's ear.

The south side was proving fruitful and my ten percent was starting to weigh down the bed. I was in the cash and a happy bunny. Finding good jobs was easy with the help of one Rachel Score - a pro from the Gorbals and Martin's snitch.

Rachel was blonde, over made up, over padded, corseted to the hilt and wore dresses that promised much if you could just figure how to release her from them. She let Martin know when houses were going to be empty and in turn she earned a cut of the take. Martin also paid her a little extra, in return for some extra marital exercise that Mrs Sketchmore was unaware of. As to me I never got a sniff of Rachel's charms. Martin saw to that.

'Don't get involved with the tart. She'll turn on you in a second.'

That didn't stop him.

The gigs Rachel found us were easy. On a Friday night Martin would make a visit to the Gorbals, partake of Rachel, and come back with an empty ball sack; a full list of all the houses on the go for that weekend in his pocket.

All was roses and wine until, one weekend, Susan Sketchmore got her claws in and grounded Martin. In his absence I was despatched to meet the lovely Rachel with strict instructions to pick up the list and nothing else - chance would be a fine thing.

I met Rachel in the pre-arranged close only to find her giving one of her regulars a knee trembler. Without pausing she reached into her handbag, took out a piece of paper and handed it to me. If her 'friend' noticed I was there he never gave a sign. I left to the sound of a deep grunt as her customer finished his business.

Once back on the street I was tempted to look at the list but, around me the Gorbals was alive with eyes and ears and it wasn't until I got home that I scanned the list of names and addresses.

All, bar one, were alien to me. The familiar name was David Read.

I knew David's dad of old. He had been a big customer of my old engineering company and a man with contacts at Ford. Money was not an issue but he was a Gorbals man through and through and wasn't for moving to some fancy detached house in the suburbs. Over the years he had purchased every flat in his close. A bit of cash to the council and a front door appeared where the communal entrance had once been. Then he set about converting the whole building into the home of his dreams.

The old man had died the year before and David now had a four-floor house with nine rooms to a floor and more toilets than was good for a man.

Read's name was removed from the list - it wasn't going to Martin – this one was for me.

I re-wrote the list in my best forged handwriting and Martin and I spent the weekend emptying valuables from homes.

On the Sunday night Martin called it quits around ten and told me we should both get going while the going was good. I made my excuses and told him I was walking into town for a drink. He shrugged his shoulders and told me to pass by his house the next morning for my share and left. I waited until he was well gone and then some.

Chapter 6

The Read's house was down near the river and by the time I got to it, it was nearer twelve than eleven. The front door was flush to the main wall. This meant no shadow to work in. If someone walked along the street, I would stick out like a sore thumb. I needed to work quickly and I needed to be lucky.

I remember standing at the corner of the street looking at the front door wondering what lay behind it. All weekend we had lifted cheap jewellery and cash. The jewellery would be fenced by one of Martin's friends for a fraction of its worth and for three nights' work the amount of cash would seem poor.

I knew that, had I given the Read's address to Martin it would have been first and if the pickings had been rich there would have been no need to scrape away the hard earned belongings of the Gorbals poor further down the list.

I had to hope that there was a jackpot behind the door. Not least because I knew my deception would be discovered – Rachel wouldn't forget to ask Martin how he had fared with a house like the Reads. All I could hope for was a score big enough to free me of Martin and set me up on my own.

That was, is, and always will be my problem. Nothing was ever enough. I always wanted more and I always wanted more far quicker than made sense.

In my life I wanted round the corner before I had reached the end of the street. I wanted over the next hill before I'd climbed the one in front of me. Tomorrow was too late, today was a touch tardy and yesterday meant I already had it and didn't want it anymore.

To add to my drive I felt the world owed me something for taking my mum and dad away. Some big fucking favour that I was entitled to call in whenever I needed it. There had to be an upside to losing your parents, even if one of them had pissed your life away at the feet of horses that were never quick enough.

As I waited in the still of that night I thought this is my time. A time for change. Come morning, I'll be a new person. Fresh out of the wrapper. The past buried in the dustbin with my last packet of Golden Wonder.

I remember the wind on my face as if it was carrying a new soul for me to try on. Wrapping me in a warm blanket of optimism.

I was so right and I was so wrong – a two-edged simultaneous equation.

Chapter 7

I stood at that corner of the Read's road for an hour before deciding the moment was right.

I slid along on the opposite side of the street like a limpet, eyes peeled, ears wide open. A man emerged from a close further down the street and I froze but he turned away and I saw the cloud of breath follow him as he hurried against the growing cold.

With a last look up and down the street I crossed to the door, pulling out my toolkit as I walked.

I had now acquired a regular locksmith's wallet of assorted picks and files. I removed one of the picks from the wallet and, as I reached the door, bent down and slid it into the keyhole. I pulled a second pick from the wallet and pushed it in beside its brother.

Back then I didn't know any of the technical jargon that goes with picking locks. Pins, shells, hubs and plates meant nothing. I just moved around bits of metal and if I was lucky opened the lock. The street faded from my mind and all my effort focussed on springing the lock. If someone came along now it was too late to do anything else but try and open the door and make it look like I was supposed to be there.

The lock turned out to be a penny drop – my name for the easy ones. Why penny drop – well when I was scavenging as a kid one of the favourite scams was to drop a penny in front of someone. When they bent over to pick it up, me and my mates would rush them, push them over and grab their bag, wallet, purse, coat – you name it. It was an easy way to earn if you had the balls and could run.

The lock clicked, I flicked the handle and I was in.

It was dark as sin in that house. I closed the door and the noise echoed along the walls. Clearly the close was still lined with tiles. I thought the Reads would have decorated the hall – to make it more like part of the home but it smelled and sounded like a thousand other closes across the city.

It was only then that I realised how ill equipped I was for the job. I had no torch. Martin always brought his along. I had no idea where to start looking either. Remember this used to be a building that housed fourteen families over four levels. Where the hell would the bedrooms be - always a good start point when doing over a house.

But I was in and I wasn't going back. Strike that - I couldn't go back. I either made this job pay or Martin would be over me like a rash. A little extra cash from this job and maybe I could hire some muscle to keep him at bay.

I ran my fingers along the close wall as I walked, feeling the cool of the ceramic surface on my fingers.

I reached the bottom of the stairwell and tried the first door. It opened easily and, as I stepped in, I could smell the bleach and fat fighting – the kitchen.

I backed out and closed the door, crossed to the other side and pushed at another door. My nose caught the whiff of stale cigar smoke and through thick curtains enough light played to show me that this flat had been turned into one giant room. I walked forward and felt wood under my feet. I saw the shape of an armchair near one of the windows and, at the far side, I saw the glint of something. I walked across the wood and froze. A shape moved in the dark.

I tilted my head a few inches to the left and the shape moved again. I froze again. I could make out the rough shape of a man or a woman. I shifted my head again and the shape's head copied me and I let out a laugh. Walking forward I touched the ice chill of a mirror and breathed a sigh of relief. I traced the mirror all the way to the window and then all the way back to the far wall. I reached up and I couldn't feel the top of it. It stretched all the way to the ground.

I had heard of such rooms in dance classes but I had never been in one. It took a fair bit of cash to buy someone's house just to turn it into a dance studio. I looked over at the armchair and wondered if the old man used to sit and watch the dancers practising. I shivered – there was something not quite right with that thought.

I retraced my steps and walked back into the stair well. I was fascinated by the whole place. Why would someone buy an entire tenement with all the cost of converting it? It was a massive undertaking. David's dad must have really loved the Gorbals.

I started up the stairs hoping that common sense would put the living rooms on the next floor and, at worst, the bedrooms on the floor above. If the bedrooms were at the top of the building I was in for a long search.

At the next floor there should have been three doors leading off the landing. Instead there was one door right at the top of the stairs and when I pushed it open there was carpet beneath my feet.

The light was better up there. The three homes on this floor had been opened up into a huge living area with windows on three sides. If the dance studio was impressive the scale here was breathtaking.

Here was a man who had a living room the size of three houses. Around me there was a wealth of furniture and I wondered if it was safe to turn on a light. I could see some lamps and given the curtains were shut I decided to risk it and, after some fumbling, I managed to switch on a small table lamp.

The room hove into view and it was no less impressive - although I couldn't help wondering how the hell three families had managed to live their lives in the space.

The walls were a veritable art gallery of paintings. In those days I had no idea of the value of such art. I studied a few and thought I could do better given half a chance and a bunch of crayons. Of course I was so wrong it hurts.

I crossed the room and scanned for anything of value and my eyes found a chest with a gold padlock the size of a loaf of bread. It was the sort of chest that you would expect to see in Treasure Island. The padlock could only mean one thing – jackpot.

I took out my lock pick kit and popped the padlock with ease. I raised the lid and jewellery shone in the dim light. The chest was stuffed with it. If it was real I could retire today and six generations of my descendants would never run out of cash.

It was then that my life took a left turn. I suddenly knew that I was in the wrong place. I slammed the lid down and locked the padlock. I sprinted across the room, dousing the light as I went and I was down and out the front door like the wind across the top of Ben Nevis.

As I ran I knew I was in the deep brown stuff. Deep in the crapper. I knew what I had to do but my guts were churning and I wanted to be sick.

It was well after one o'clock by then but that made no difference. I knew where David Read might be and I now knew what he was - and more importantly what he could do.

I cut down on to the Clydeside, across the Albert Bridge and headed with speed towards the Merchant City.

I found the street I was looking for - gasping for breath and scared to the bottom of my nuts.

Chapter 8

The single light above the door told me I had arrived at the right place. I walked up to it, paused, took a deep breath and knocked on the imposing double door that guarded the entrance.

High up in the wood a small shutter slid back and a pair of eyes looked down on me.

'Mr Read, please.'

I said it in a whisper but it was enough. The left hand door swung open and heat and light spilled onto the street.

'And what would a little gob-shite like you be wanting with Mr Read?'

The doorman was decked out in a royal blue overcoat that struggled to keep his muscles in check. This was no polite club steward. This man was a human blockade.

'Tell him that someone is going to do his house over.'

The blockade cocked his head and vanished.

I tell you now that I wanted to run. With every bone in my body I wanted to sprint down that street and let the night swallow me up. I'll also tell you that had I done so I would have been dead in twenty-four hours and you wouldn't be here listening to this.

Two men in dark suits appeared in the doorway and, without stopping for a by your leave, stepped onto the pavement, lifted me bodily by the armpits and whisked me along the road and into St Andrews Square.

They hauled me round the church that sits in the centre of the square and into the shadows beyond. I was dumped to the ground and one of the men kicked me in the thigh.

Just making his point.

I lay on the cold pavement and waited. I knew better than to ask any questions. Questions led to pain.

I looked up at the church and from the back end of my mind I remembered being told that Bonnie Prince Charlie's army had encamped around the church's walls after the disastrous invasion of England in 1745. I think I knew how he felt.

The two suits lit up cigarettes but said nothing and I watched as the crappy street lighting played games with the smoke.

I heard footsteps and a heavily over coated man rounded the corner. He was stocky and walked with purpose. A man used to getting his own way in life. The two suits parted and he walked up to me.

'Stand up.'

I did as I was asked and he turned and told the suits to take a walk. Obviously I was no threat.

'I'm here. Talk.'

I launched into my story. Disjointed and without purpose he looked bored until I told him about my break in to his house and his eyes darkened. I told him I had taken nothing and seen nothing. His eyes dropped another shade. He didn't believe me.

I told him where I had got the info on the house and I told him I was in the shit however this played out.

'How did Rachel Score know that I wouldn't be home tonight?'

I shrugged.

'How did you know to find me at the club?'

'I didn't but I knew your dad used it. If you hadn't been here I'd have left a message for you to contact me.'

He laughed. It sounded odd in the dark. But I could see his point. Me leave a message for him – good joke.

'So why don't I just get my friends to teach you to swim with a chain round your legs?'

I tell you my heart was racing at twenty to the dozen and then some. I had no plan other than to offer up Martin and Rachel in return for my safety.

'Because if I hadn't come here Martin would have done over your house. Still might.'

He looked at me. The way a boy looks at a bug just before he squashes it. He shouted back to one of the suits for a cigarette and, as he lit up, he never let his eyes stray from mine.

'Your not as daft as you look,' he said. 'Any other boy would have either trashed the house or run. But you figured you were dead meat either way. Not bad. What did you see that told you not to fuck with me?'

I didn't want to talk about the chest but I did. As soon as I saw it I knew that Read was not someone to mess with. There was serious shit in that chest and that meant someone who was a lot heavier than Martin and I. Much heavier.

He blew out a cloud and threw the butt to the ground.

'Tell you what. I'll give you one chance to make good. Fuck up and you're history.'

He told me what to do.

Chapter 9

Eleven fourteen and twelve seconds.

Suffice to say that night I entered the circle of Mr Read and his associates. A then unknown circle but one that was to prove a hell of a stepping stone.

I left him by the church and sprinted all the way to Martin's. I told him what I had done and made it clear he had one hour to leave town. I finished by telling him that Mr Read's friends would be paying a visit if he didn't vanish.

He flapped like a cat on a cooker ring. I may not have known who Read was but Martin did and I left with no end of threats to my person but Martin's rantings were nothing compared to the verbal abuse that Rachel Score heaped on me when I delivered her the same message. She was less restrained on the physical front and opened a gash in my cheek with a vase that was at hand.

I went home that night shaking with the adrenalin rush. I couldn't sleep and spent the night waiting for Mr Read, the suits, Martin or Rachel to break down my door.

The next morning a kid of about twelve arrived at my door. I recognised him as Mary Templeton's, the wife of the local corner store's owner, youngest offspring, He pushed a piece of paper into my hand and ran off.

The paper had a time and place on it – nothing else. Three o'clock. Hillhead Underground station.

I turned up half an hour early and hung around until one of the suits from the previous evening appeared and gave me another note. It was from Mr Read and I now had a new boss.

The next few years were a turning point for me. After a few months of thinning my shoe leather, Mr Read's right hand man, a brutal beast called Craig Laidlaw, sussed out I had a talent for breaking and entering. He watched me at work a few times and, quite rightly, ranked me as nothing more than a talented amateur. He sent me to meet a man called Kelly Greenlaw.

Kelly was an ex-housebreaker well into retirement, who now spent as much time as possible staring at the bottom of an empty whisky glass in the local pub.

In his day he had been the dog's bollocks as a burglar and now earned his dram money as a part time professor and tutor in the art of breaking and entering.

When I first met him he said nothing until I bought him a nip. It transpired that this was how things worked. I bought whisky and he opened up a little.

Kelly was an expensive tutor. When we graduated to hands on practical work I was expected to buy a quarter bottle from the Stockwell Off Sales. He watched as I jimmied locks, cracked window catches and smashed and trashed what couldn't be picked. If I took too long I was despatched to the off sales for a second bottle.

To earn cash to feed Kelly's habit I went back to loan collection for Mr Read but I didn't mind. Kelly might have been an out and out alcoholic but he knew his stuff.

Then, one day, after a trip to the pub, Kelly took me to meet a couple of men up a back alley off Argyll Street in the centre of Glasgow.

I was presented with a door and made mince meat of it in seconds. Once inside we all climbed two floors and I was shown another door. I cracked it and we entered an office dominated by a row of mesh-protected windows, each with a customer slot. Each slot was attended by a till with its drawer wide open - empty for the world to see.

Kelly nodded at the far wall and to another door. This one was different. For a start it was made of metal and build into a steel frame. There was also the matter of two keyholes and a padlock - all keeping its contents nice and secure. Kelly pushed me forward.

It took a little longer for me to crack it but we were in soon enough. This seemed to impress my colleagues.

The room beyond was wall to ceiling with shelving. Each shelf was stuffed with paper. I pulled out one of the bits of paper and recognised it as a betting slip. That explained the windows and tills. This was a back street bookie's shop.

In the centre of the floor stood a small safe bolted to the floor. It looked new and solid and reminded me of the safe at Malcolm Smillie's place. Kelly grunted and got to his knees. I stepped back but was pushed forward by one of Kelly's friends and sat down next to the safe. It was clear I was here to learn.

Kelly walked me through what he was doing; downing the obligatory quarter bottle as he did so.

He explained how the safe worked and what we needed to listen for. I thought the stethoscope he used was a joke but, back then, safes really could be cracked by listening for the tumblers falling.

He popped it open and I stood up, expecting the men to empty the contents but Kelly closed the door, spun the tumbler and handed me the stethoscope.

It took me three minutes – a good ten quicker than Kelly to crack it. He was impressed. Mr Read had the need of a good safe cracker and I had just pulled on the team strip.

That was the last night I saw Kelly. He vanished and turned up in the King George V dock a week later. Nobody suspected foul play. I reckon he just got tired of life and went for a swim – blind drunk. But I always wondered if my little demonstration in the bookies had been the straw that had broken his booze-soaked back.

Mr Read worked me hard. I was hardly an expert at my craft and I had no choice but to learn as I went. At first my jobs were far from Glasgow. With a varying set of companions I travelled the length and breadth of the country – Newcastle, Liverpool, Cardiff, Manchester, Derby, Carlisle, Plymouth – the list was endless.

Each time the routine was the same. I would get my orders via Mary's kid and meet a variation of my new friends at Central Station. They would have the destination, tickets and a carry-out.

On arrival at the town of choice we would meet up with some locals in a dingy pub. Always a dingy pub. They would explain the gig and point us in the right direction. Job done we never hung around and, on the occasions that we could not get the last train out, there would be a car to take us home. For two years I saw the UK by night.

After a while I realised that we never touched London and I once asked why, only to be told to mind my own fucking business.

A year later I found out why.

With my cash flow improving I had moved out of my flat and bought a semi-detached house on the south side. Nothing too grand but I was on the up. The jobs were regular and so far trouble free. I wasn't high enough up to get the big cut, but I got a fair wage and my skills as a safe cracker were growing.

By now Mary's kid had given way to the phone and when I received a call to go to the train station I packed my bag as usual and met up with two of Mr Read's elder statesmen - George Cummings and Tony Wright.

George and Tony were heavyweights and usually reserved for big jobs. I'd never been with them on a gig before. When we boarded the London train I knew this was something different.

The journey south was done in near silence. George and Tony slept most of the way. The silence made me nervous and I didn't close an eye for the whole journey.

When we pulled in at Euston, I was exhausted and they looked fresh. This time there were no locals and no dingy pub. We took a taxi and jumped out near the Albert Hall and checked into one of the myriad of small hotels that surround it. I had never been to London before but was destined to see little on this trip.

Once in the hotel room George and Tony got to work on the phone and told me to get some shuteye. I thought I was still too uptight to sleep but must have dozed off because around three in the morning I was woken by Tony and told to get ready.

We left by the front door. The receptionist was long in bed and, back then, night watchmen were a luxury few small hotels needed or could afford – so no one saw us leave. We hailed a taxi and headed south and over the River Thames.

I remember being surprised at how quiet the streets were. I had always imagined London to be a 24/7 sort of place but around us the streets were more alive with rubbish than people.

We reached an industrial district and got out of the taxi. George took a battered A to Z from his pocket and orientated himself before plunging us into a maze of canyons created by warehouse walls. For twenty minutes we wandered, sometimes backtracking until Tony pointed at a small two storey building. George nodded and we crossed the road, all the time keeping our eyes open for signs of life.

There was a double door to the building - I didn't need to be asked and went straight to work on the lock and cracked it in seconds. A set of stairs faced us, leading up to the second floor, and my services were required again at the top.

We stepped into a barnyard of a place. Steel columns stretched into the distance like soldiers on parade. In between the columns there were long stretches of workbenches, each attended by row upon row of stools. At the far end there was a small smattering of offices and we made for the last one.

It was locked but, before I could pull the locksmith's kit from my pocket, George picked up a block of wood from a nearby table and put it through the glass in the door.

Inside I was faced with a steel door on the far wall, not unlike the one in the bookies that I had cut my teeth on. I set to work and once inside I had expected to find a safe but, instead, the room contained rows of small boxes built into the wall, floor to ceiling, each with its own keyhole. I had never seen inside a bank vault but I thought this is what the safety deposit room would look like.

I asked which box we were after and George shrugged and told me to do them all. I gasped - there were easily two hundred boxes and, outside, the light was moving from night to dawn.

I started on my left and it took a few minutes to pop the first one but once I had the measure of the locks, the rest fell with ease. Even so it took over an hour before George called Tony over and examined the contents of the latest box I had opened.

They removed what lay inside and told me to call it quits and we made for the exit and this is when the world went south.

Chapter 10

As we exited the office the first sign of trouble barrelled into the work area in the shape of four men, three armed with crowbars and one with a sawn off baseball bat. They were at one end of the workspace and we were at the other.

As soon as George saw them he reached into his coat, took out the package from the safety deposit box and handed it to me.

'That way,' he pointed to a fire escape. 'We'll take care of this.'

I didn't argue. The intruders were eating up ground between us like cheetahs on heat. I put my head down and ran. Behind me there was a brief silence and then a grunt as wood connected with flesh and bone.

I hit the fire escape door at full tilt but in the seventies quick release fire doors were still to be introduced, and I bounced off it - ending up on my backside. The noise behind me was racking up and I grabbed a quick look see.

George and Tony were holding centre stage. George with a cosh that I knew he kept in his jacket and Tony with a lump of two by two he had ripped from a table.

I returned my attention to the door, realised my mistake, flipped the door handle and was gone. Dropping down the metal staircase onto the alley below I struggled to get my bearings, so I mentally flipped a coin and began running.

Soon I was swallowed by the warehouse labyrinth and, after a while my energy levels fell off, forcing me to drop to a walk. I was heaving in air but still kept some pace on. It took me an hour to find my way back to the main road and another twenty minutes to get a cab.

My instructions were simple. If we were split up we were to meet up at Euston Station and if no one was there I was to jump the first train to Glasgow.

Euston was quiet. It was over an hour until the first train was due north and I bided my time by wandering between the toilets and a side entrance - trying to keep a low profile.

With five minutes to go there was still no sign of George and Tony and I boarded the train bathed in sweat.

I breathed deeply as it pulled out of the station.

The journey was long and full of questions but no-one to ask them of. When the train pulled into Glasgow I headed straight for Craig Laidlaw. I took him to one side and told him what had gone down. I handed him the package and he told me to 'fuck off' for a while.

Three days later London invaded Glasgow.

I never saw it but I heard plenty. Some of it is now legend. Bar fights, street brawls, one on ones and even shooters. The guys from London were good and well used to a fight but this was home turf for Mr Read and before the day was out the London gang had turned tail and fled.

I was summoned to a rare meet with the victor. He told me I had done well. I thought I had turned chicken by running - go figure. George and Tony were on their way back up - a bit of a mess but they would live.

London was pissed off, Mr Read was basking in it all and I was dying to ask what was in the package that had kicked all this off - but I didn't have the nerve to ask.

As it turned out I didn't need to. Mr Read reached into his pocket and took out the small cloth pack that I had carried from London. He opened it up and the world was full of glinting light.

Diamonds, dozens and dozens of diamonds lying in the palm of his hand. I knew nothing of their value but the smile on Mr Read's face told a story. He reached into the pile, picked out two and handed them to me.

'Joey will sort you out when you want to trade them in.'

He patted me on the head like a kid, wrapped up the gems and was gone. I was twenty five and I felt like a ten year old. I had just been handed near on a grand's worth of diamonds.

It was time to move on.

Chapter 11

My step into the big time was not an easy one and I could fill the remaining time we have together with stories of woe and times that were hard. Of how I had to struggle to rise above the mob and sacrifice my every want and desire as I strove for a brighter future. I could but I won't. I'll keep to the real juice.

It was late August and the Scottish summer had been the usual mix of pish and rotten. I was recovering from a late one at the Griffin - my new pub of choice and witness to a quiet night out to celebrate a nice haul from a job in Edinburgh.

The next morning I was sitting nursing my head thinking that the share from the London job would put a nice dent in my mortgage when the doorbell rang. I rose expecting to find the postman trying to force fit an unwanted catalogue into my letterbox. Instead I found two men, neither of whom I had laid eyes on before, standing on my doorstep.

They were polite and well dressed and I guessed them for Jehovah's Witnesses. I told them I was Buddhist but they politely smiled and asked if they could come in. I refused and the smaller of the two reached into his jacket pocket and pulled out a gun.

I let them in.

They asked for a cup of tea and I felt it would be a wise move to acquiesce and returned ten minutes latter with two brews and a plate of digestives. They sat and sipped the tea without a word.

I waited, assuming there was a point to the visit. I wasn't unduly worried about the gun. If they had intended to kill me the job would have been done by now.

'Do you enjoy working for Mr Read?'

The man with the gun's accent was laced with a southern lilt.

I didn't answer.

'Smart kid,' said the other. 'Nice tea as well.'

The man with the gun leant forward.

'We have a proposition but there's no going back once you've heard it.'

Cryptic. My interest was piqued.

'Do you want us to go on?' said the gunman

'Depends?'

'It is in your interest,' said the other.

'Are you sure?'

'Yip,' said the gunman.

'Then proceed.'

'Good,' said the other.

A right Laurel and Hardy double act.

'You'll be aware of the little incident that took place recently in relation to some unwarranted activity in London by your Mr Read. Well we represent a business that is looking to expand into Scotland. We foresee a small opportunity in this neck of the woods and our clients feel that the recent unpleasantness could have been easily avoided. We are looking for bright capable people who could help us.'

It didn't take Einstein to figure out what kind of business they represented.

'We are aware of the standing of Mr Read, and his activities represent a bit of a barrier to our expansion plans. We know you are a loyal employee of Mr Read and...'

He looked around the room.

'... you seem to be doing ok.'

He made the words 'doing ok' sound like 'doing shite'.

'Our client,' he continued, 'has given us permission to make an offer for you to join our firm. You would become our number two in Scotland and report to the new head of Scottish affairs. In return we will cut you in for a share of the total Scottish pie. Five percent to be exact. With a following wind we expect to clear one million in our first year.'

I did the maths as the gunman sat back to let me take this in. I had just been offered fifty thousand pounds a year as if it were a packet of soor plums from the corner store. I had enough sense to keep my mouth shut. For all I knew this was some bizarre loyalty test by Mr Read.

'We don't expect an answer right away but it may help your decision to know that Mr Read will be heading for some choppy waters. He would have been well advised to stay clear of the capital. Our offer is valid for twenty four hours and you can get me on this number.'

He threw a card across the table. It was blank save for a Glasgow phone number.

'We would also look upon any conversation with Mr Read or his associates about this meeting as an unwise act on your part.'

With that they got up and left. I stared at the card wondering what the hell that was all about.

Chapter 12

To say I was confused was a major understatement. I was hardly a king pin in Mr Read's organisation and, as such, I suspected that the visit might indeed be a test of some sort.

I decided to phone Craig Laidlaw. I had no idea what I was going to say but I needed to start somewhere – you don't turn down a fifty grand until you're sure the offer is a turkey.

Craig was in a bad mood. That is to say his usual mood.

'What the fuck do you want?' he growled down the line.

I asked if there were any more jobs coming up as I was thinking of taking a short break. Craig laughed at this.

'Off for a shag in Spain?'

I laughed back.

'No jobs I know of but there is some weird shit going down.'

I asked what, but he wouldn't elaborate.

'Let me check with the boss before you start packing the condoms.'

The phone rang an hour later.

'The boss said he wants no-one out of town for the next couple of weeks.'

I asked why?

'Something *is* going down but that's all I know.'

He was lying. Craig was Brutus to Caesar and knew a damn sight more than he let on.

'What about a trip doon the watter?' I asked.

'Zip.' he said. 'Get the message. Nothing. Not even a night at the pictures. Stock up on art mags and curry, and stay put until I call.'

Things were looking interesting and I had no intention of staying in doors, so I set the answer machine and put on my jacket. The machine could be operated remotely from another phone. If Craig phoned I would know and could get back double quick.

I headed for the only person I could think of.

Martin Sketchmore's face was a picture when I swanned up to his front door. He had only just returned after his forced absence of leave. One of Mr Read's cronies had told me he was back home.

He slammed the door on me but I hung on to the doorbell like a leech until he gave in and let me in. I didn't bother with small talk and told him what had happened (minus the monetary offer) and he looked at me with his head at an angle that must have hurt.

'What the hell are you telling me for? Why would I give a rat's shit?'

'You want to get back at Read?'

He tilted his head the other way.

'What kind of question is that? I'm not stupid. It's taken me all this time to come home. Why would I want to screw it up again? Anyway why shouldn't I go to him and tell him about our little chat. I'm sure he would be more than interested to find out why you haven't told him?'

'Because he won't take a call from you,' I said. 'Because if this is true you'd be stupid not to be interested. Because I know he has your balls in a sling and is asking for fifty percent of your earnings in return for letting you live. Because he has lined up a world shattering set of crap jobs for you to do. Because if you were to get caught in any one of those jobs it is a minimum of two years in Bar L. Now what do you know about a new mob on the scene?'

Martin turned away and looked out the window. Things had been tough since his exile but I'd heard that he had started to run with a gang from London and I was betting there was some word on the street about a move north.

'Rumours,' he said.

'Like what?'

'I'm not sure. It started about a year ago. Rumours of a new boss on the scene. The guys I was working with put it down to the same old, same old. There's always gossip on the go. Stories of some new king muscling in. Hot air and nonsense most of the time.'

'So what changed?'

'Eddie Haliburton.'

I knew of Eddie. Most people in our game did. A major player down south. Old school. Friend of the Krays and all that.

'He'd died a while back. Car crash somewhere in the sticks,' I said.

'Spot on. Only thing was that he was found with no head. Nothing to do with the crash. It would seem that Eddie got in the car – minus his head, which would make steering difficult, drove into a tree and the petrol tank exploded'

'Anything else.'

'Chuck Semple.'

Another name I knew and another dead man.

'Went swimming in a DJ in St Catherine's dock.'

'And? Were they connected?'

'Rumour mill says so. Add to that about half a dozen of both Eddie's and Chuck's senior crew going missing and you can see a pattern.'

'Fuck. That's serious shit.'

'Could be. Might just be a turf war. I left London before Chuck went for a dip so I'm a little out of touch.'

I knew how hard it had been for Martin to come home. He'd offered up a raft of future favours to Mr Read before he was allowed back. Read had taken his offers and tripled them. Martin was in for a few years full of crap. No wonder he was opening up. I represented a way out.

'So why would they approach me. I'm hardly in Read's inner circle.'

'Story goes,' he says, 'that this new mob don't want the old guard when they move into an area. Too unreliable. Too likely to rebel. They don't need thinkers, just doers. Foot soldiers they can mould. If they are coming to Scotland then you fit the bill.'

'Me?'

'Take Jack Rushent. He worked for Eddie. Low level but bright. A month after Eddie and his team vanish Jack suddenly has money on his hip and has moved up a social circle or two. He's about your age and was about your level.'

I mulled this over.

'Look,' said Martin. 'I think you've just been made an offer you can't refuse.'

49

'How do you figure? It could be Read checking me out.'

'Could be - but unlikely. If someone is moving in, Read has far better things to do than check up on every grunt in the team. Besides what would he learn? That some of his trusted men were willing to jump sides for a wedge. Hardly a revelation is it? I think the offer is genuine.'

'So what do I do?'

'Why ask me?'

'Because I think you know more than you are letting on.'

Martin closed his eyes and shook his head - loosing the cobwebs.

'Tell you what,' he said. 'You cut me in for a cut of your cut and I'll help you out.'

'What about Read?'

'If this is really going down I'd rather be on the winning side. He was an idiot with the job in London. From what I hear he is history, with a motorway support as a grave in his near future. But you're going to have to be plenty smart if you want to get through this intact. If Read gets wind you are on the flip he'll nail your balls to the City Chambers.'

I wanted time to think but I knew my decision. Martin was right. Hobson's choice.

A day later I offered him twenty percent of my cut and he agreed. I phoned the number on the piece of paper and was told to go to Tennents Bar in Byres Rd in the west end of Glasgow. I told them about Martin and was asked to bring him along. They didn't seem bothered about him.

I was to meet a man carrying a copy of the Daily Telegraph. Brave man - that could get you killed in some pubs in Glasgow back then.

I turned up with Martin in tow and we were bundled into a car and driven to a small flat in Yoker. We were told to cool our heels in the flat for forty-eight hours and we would be contacted. We had no guards but it was clear what would happen if we stepped outside the door.

Two days later and David Read was headline news on Scotland Today when his body was found in a coalbunker behind a small hotel on the south side. We later found out that he had been discovered with a dick in his mouth. Not his own but Craig Laidlaw's. Craig's body was found on wasteland near the Clyde and three other known associates of Read's were declared permanently AWOL.

On the third night the gunman and his mate reappeared and told us how it was going to be. We didn't have much choice so went along for the ride.

Chapter 13

You would think that my life was full of the cloak and dagger nonsense back then and, to be fair, it sometimes felt like that. But most of the time I just put my head down and got on with life. True I was no nine to five guy but I looked on work as work and that way kept my head screwed on – at least for a while.

As soon as we were dropped off at the Albany Hotel I knew things were changing for the better.

How did I know this?

Simple really. Full length leather jacketed, jewellery-laden guys with bottle blondes on each arm don't walk up to me every day and say 'Welcome aboard son.'

I was ushered into the hotel lobby, whisked to the top floor and shown into a suitably plush suite. Martin and I were herded into one corner, handed a large whisky and told to chill.

I often wondered what was going through Martin's head back then. Maybe you would know?

No?

Well time to move on.

Mr Leather dropped the blondes on a chair and flipped them a bottle of champagne and a couple of glasses. The girls were all fur coat and nae knickers but the way they got to work on the champagne showed they were no strangers to the good life.

Our driver lifted me by the elbow and led me to the next room where Mr Leather was stripping to a Saville Row suit and an outrageously out of date kipper tie.

He motioned for me to take a seat and the driver dropped another three fingers of malt into my glass.

'Names don't matter son,' said Mr Leather. 'You won't see me again.'

He stood at the far end of the room and I noted that his hair seemed to have a life of its own. Expensive wig. A crap one but expensive. Add to that the way the fat round his waist failed to move with him and I suspected that a twenty-four hour Playtex was de rigueur for my new leather coated friend.

'I'll keep it short,' he said. 'Life's changing. Small time gangs are on their way out. Think big, that's the secret. This is nearly the eighties and we need to change. Take your Mr Read. Nice operator - until he pulled that diamond stunt. Wrong job, wrong place and no thought to the future. Hard to think that he expected us to let a million quids worth of ice just walk.'

A million and all I got was a lousy grand.

'Glasgow wasn't high on the list for us but your Mr Read changed that. A bit of research and a bit of planning and here we are.'

He paused to sip at the beer he had just poured.

'Anyway new management needs new personnel. Personnel with ambition and drive. Word goes you're not half daft and a whizz at the old safes. So, we say to ourselves, we need someone with a bit of nonce and cool under pressure. You seem to fit the bill, so here's the script. We set you up in an office. None too grand but nice – if you know where I'm coming from. We give you a contact and he passes on a few errands we need done. You help us out and we cut you in for five percent of the action.'

'You're going to need some help. I'm assuming that is why your friend is here. It's up to you how you fund the help. We don't mind a few homers but nothing that will get you noticed. Keep it under the radar and we will be fine.'

'Give us twelve months unblemished service and we double your cut in year two.'

He took another slug of beer.

'It is about here that you expect me to say 'any questions?' but it isn't going to happen. You are a smart kid. There is no negotiation on this unless you want to negotiate over the colour of your wreath.'

'Get the picture?'

He finished the beer.

'Time for me to go. The pros next doors are yours to do what with what you want. The room is paid up until tomorrow and the tab on room service is open for light refreshments but not for abuse.'

He headed for the adjoining door.

'We'll be in touch.'

And with that he was gone. I got up and followed him through but save the two girls and Martin, the room was empty.

We had a hell of a night. The girls were willing and more than able and the bar tab was large but at the back of my head I knew that there was no such thing as a free lunch and my new life might include a touch more than 'a few errands'.

Chapter 14

Two days later a bruiser of a man turned up at my door and handed me a set of keys that were dripping with the grease from his just finished fish supper along with a letter, crumpled and battered. Hardly the auspicious start to the new life I had been expecting.

Inside the letter was a slip of paper with an address and the words – 'Move in and wait.'

The keys turned out to open an office on Gordon St that lay four floors above a Chinese restaurant. It shared a common entrance with the Chinky's (you could call it that back then) and in the following year we had a line of credit with the restaurant that made us their best customers by a country mile.

The office itself was a simple two room affair. One room was set out as a reception with a desk and a battered two-seat sofa that attended a plywood coffee table. The next room had a desk, chair and a filing cabinet that didn't work. Decoration was from the late grime period and two forty-watt light bulbs provided some gloom. The view - a trade description violation in itself - was of a brick wall.

I made my first executive decision and, dipping into my own pocket, I called in a girl called Sally Macintyre. Sally was an interior decorator – one of the few in Glasgow in the late seventies. She usually did the houses of the rich and not so famous. I gave her a free hand, a small budget and told her I needed the place to look business like with an air of authority.

Two weeks later I had the smartest office in the west of Scotland but still no contact from London.

When it eventually came it seemed innocent enough at first.

Most of the early jobs were simple pick and drops and I pulled together a team of runners under the watchful eye of Martin.

Glasgow's waifs and strays flowed through our offices, turning it into an all day rush hour. The office was always alive with activity. We went from one to six phones - that raised a few eyes with the GPO - we were still a year short of the creation of British Telecom. Within a month I had rented the office next door and knocked through - creating an area for the pick and drop crew - named the PD's by Martin. We put in a coffee and tea machine and, eventually, a telly, radio and a hot plate.

The first big job came three months in and it was a darling.

A bruiser appeared at our office and handed me a distressed envelope - clearly London specialised in the battered look. It contained a date and a time.

I made the rendezvous outside a chippie on Dumbarton Rd thirty minutes before I needed to. It was a habit back then - turning up early - it let me suss out if there was going to be nonsense. The meet was short and I was given another envelope.

The gig was a new one on me. Kidnapping. The letter gave me a name and an address. The objective of the exercise was a warning to a businessman who was not paying up on the protection front. Normally this was a knee cap job but London wanted to make a different mark this time and I was told to lift the business man's six year old, and not to hand the kid back until the protection money started flowing.

For the record I added in ten grand to the demands - strictly for my back pocket.

I lifted the kid from school and took him to a flat that I had rented for the month.

To say I was an amateur at this was as big an understatement as could be made about me back then. For a start I had no food or drink in the flat. Naively I had assumed that the businessman would come up with the goods in hours and I would be out of there post haste. What I hadn't banked on was that he was currently in Spain, banging his heart out with his private secretary.

I contacted his wife and she was hysterical but hardly in a place to stump up the readies. She wasn't aware that her husband was in the protection paying business, Spain or his secretary.

It took two days to get the message to Spain and for him to return. Meanwhile I had a six year old with the appetite of King Kong and the attention span of a newt. On half a dozen occasions I considered throwing the wee shit in the Clyde and being done with it.

When I eventually handed him over to his dad at Kelvingrove Park - it didn't matter that he saw us, he knew who we were and we knew who he was - I was so glad to get rid of the wee gobshite that I failed to count the cash. It was a grand light but by then I didn't give a rat's arse and I was well rid of the horror child.

The next year took on a turbo charged feel. The 'errands' grew in length, complexity and risk but I was up for the challenge. I shifted office after less than six months, as my needs outgrew the space, and took up residence in an old townhouse on Argyle Street.

I hit a new problem that I hadn't had to deal with to date: what to do with the mounting pile of cash I was building. Now that might sound like a good problem but it wasn't. Opening a bank account back then was a lot less rigorous than it is now but it was still folly to advertise a sudden rise in income. The Inland Revenue would take more than a passing interest in the discrepancy between what I declared and what I was bringing in. A discrepancy of enormous proportions, may I add.

The solution came in the form of Terry Usher; a disgraced banker who knew the ins and outs of the complexities of offshore banking, portfolio investment and tax avoidance. He managed a number of 'clients' and as far as I knew he hadn't rolled over on anyone yet. Still it nagged at the back of my head that he was in control of my assets and as a precaution I took to hiding some of my cash in the most obscure places.

Even now I can guarantee that there are still a few wedges lying around in my old haunts. For all I know there could be thousands.

Probably more.

Eleven twenty eight and ten seconds.

Got to keep my foot down.

Success bred success and I was on a serious roll. Job after job was thrown at me and I met each one head on and delivered. My staff grew and before the year was out we had twenty-seven on the payroll.

By year two we were up to sixty and I was no longer involved in the small jobs.

During all this time the chain of command from London didn't change. We still received the 'errands' and we had little direct contact with our masters.

Our next big move was Edinburgh.

I had been told to stay clear of the Scottish capital for a number of reasons – not least that the place was as alien to me as the Amazon rain forest. London had never given me a job in Edinburgh and I was grateful as it meant staying clear of one Malcolm Morrison, known as the Major to his friends.

The Major was a well-heeled ex-financial genius who had grabbed Edinburgh the way London had grabbed Glasgow. He was highly territorial and renowned for his retribution should someone step out of line. He had the bizarre trait of wearing military gear and, as the years had progressed, so had his rank.

As far as anyone knew he had no background in the forces but there was a rumour that he had been rejected from the TA early in his life and this sat as a scar. He was never seen in public short of a uniform or insignia. It was testament to his status that he got away with it for so long.

The message came up from London that the Major was now surplus to requirements and Edinburgh was to join the empire. There was no subtlety involved in the plan of action. Exterminate with extreme prejudice. From the Major down take out the command structure and move in.

We hit in late November of 1981. The world had gone New Romantic and Martin had taken to wearing frilly cuffs on all his shirts. Twenty of us rolled into Edinburgh at midnight on the fifteenth.

We split up and played trash and burn with the Major's property before taking out everyone from the Major, down to his lieutenants. Twelve dead – all made to look like accidents. The police went ape but back then we had brave pills by the dozen and alibis as solid as the Forth Rail Bridge. Even so I spent the best part of four months being escorted from my house to the Glasgow police head office almost daily.

The police knew I was involved. I knew they knew and they knew that I knew that they knew but it made not a hill of beans without evidence and evidence was thin on the ground.

Even while I was sitting in the interview room I had arranged for two of my more trusted compadres to scope out Edinburgh and start moving in.

It wasn't easy. Chopping off the head was simple but the hydra had many more heads waiting to take charge. It took six months to whip the city into shape and even then we only had partial control, but it was enough to keep London happy and, when the police eventually backed off, I could get on with the business of making Edinburgh profitable.

Aberdeen was next, then Dundee and then the sticks. Four years it took us and an industrial amount of pain and effort.

However on the first of January 1986 I sent a message to London. It read:

'Scotland now ours – what next?'

We hadn't really conquered Scotland. Any fool could see that but we had our fingers in most pies and the major jobs didn't happen without our say.

Incredible as it might seem I was still none the wiser as to who in London was pulling the strings. I knew a lot more than I had at the outset and had been on frequent trips to meet my opposite numbers elsewhere in the country but, as to the boss, I was clueless. When I tried to discuss it with Martin, he didn't seem interested and spent increasing amounts of time on holiday or just AWOL

By then I had more money than I could reasonably spend in the rest of my life. I had banked three houses in Scotland and was an early bird in the Spanish property market.

My car had progressed from a Ford Escort 1100 Mk1 to an Aston Martin DB4 – the one James Bond uses in Goldfinger. Women littered my path but no one had tied me down yet and the job was getting easier not harder.

I distanced myself from the day to day and if things went tits up I was six or seven people away from the pain. The police would still call but apart from enjoying a cup of tea and a Bourbon biscuit there was little else they could do. It didn't stop them from trying but the better things got for business, the further from the action I flew.

Chapter 15

When the phone call came it was hardly a surprise.

'Be in London tomorrow, you've a room booked tonight in the Hilton on Park Lane. You'll be away for a while – make arrangements.'

Click.

And so I went. Martin was nowhere to be seen and I went alone.

I'm not a fan of London. Never have been. Too many people, too little space and it takes hours to get out of the bloody place to somewhere less crowded. Then again I've mates who swear by the place. Love it. Plenty to do. Plenty to see. Plenty to eat. A real buzz.

I just don't like it.

Full stop.

The Hilton was stuffed to the gunnels with Yuppies – the real deal. Early adopter mobile phone freaks. Filofax. Power suit. Braces – the whole Wall St thing in one lobby. I almost felt like I had to miss lunch to fit in.

I sat at the bar after unpacking and hated it. Sterile decoration and the yuppies got on my tits. I slipped out, glad to be free of the smell of leather and sweat. I found a small pub in the backstreets and drank myself into a good mood and then drank myself into a shit one.

I woke up the next morning with a hangover and no sense that I had earned it.

A London suit appeared around twelve and insisted I join him on a little trip north. The Ford

Sierra we travelled in was clapped out and smelled of beer and curry. I was pushed into the back seat and any notion that I harboured of being treated with some decorum, given my track record, was beginning to diminish.

We crawled through the London traffic and slogged our way onto the North Circular before cutting into the back end of Highgate and into a run down council estate. The car stopped and an outstretched finger pointed to a door that looked like it had been firebombed. The house it served didn't look much better.

I tell you now I was nervous. I was beginning to think that this was looking like my exit interview as opposed to promotion. I walked up a path strewn with empty cans of Tennent's Super and began to rack my brains for the deals I had done over the last few months. For all the money I had salted away on the side, I could think of nothing that warranted a kicking – or worse.

Before I got to the door it opened. Another suit grabbed me by the arm and pulled me in. The door slammed behind me, and it was hard not to think of a condemned man being led from his cell.

The hall was stripped of wallpaper and carpet and the sole light bulb in the ceiling was either off or didn't work. A door at the far end of the corridor opened and warm light flooded the space. I was pushed from behind and entered an altogether different world.

The occupant was obviously used to the double take that visitors went through and gave me space to let my jaw hit the ground.

Far from the expected hovel, the space around me would have graced a stately home and not put it to shame. The walls stretched double height around me and the floor space ran to the size of a basketball court. It reminded me of David Read's gaff but far nastier on the outside and far grander on the inside.

Furniture was strategically placed amongst a full gambit of statues, display cabinets and paintings mounted on easels. The carpet was so thick that it threatened to suck the shoes from my feet and the room gave out an odour that would have been at home in a Chinese opium house a hundred years ago.

Near the far wall, behind a desk with a stone top that looked like it had been hewn from Mount Everest, sat a man. His head was bent down reading a sheaf of papers in front of him. He grunted and the two suits behind me left.

Thirty seconds silence followed.

Chapter 16

'Take a seat.'

The man pointed to a chair in front of his desk. He didn't raise his head and continued to give the paper he was reading his full attention and me none. He lifted a pen, scribbled a little and shuffled the paper into a tray. He leaned back and eyes as grey as a wet Loch Lomond sky wandered over me.

'What did we take last year?'

No preamble. No small talk.

'10.6 million clear.'

'And this year?'

'12'

'Is that good?'

I thought it was fucking fantastic but it was clear that he didn't.

'Much more and we start to step on toes that will bring down a lot more heat. Most of our cash is in small amounts. That keeps the major crime boys off our back.'

He smiled. Cold.

'Nice strategy. I approve. I reckon twenty five million tops in Scotland before we have to change the way we do things.'

Twenty five. Christ that would be hard work. The organisation would have needed to double again to get close and that was a lot of organising and recruiting.

'Not your worry,' he said. 'How do you fancy south of the river.'

For a second I was lost. South of what river?

'Giles is moving north and his number two isn't up to it. I don't see anyone better for the job. That is if you fancy it?'

I knew who Giles was. Giles Taylor and he ran south London. That meant I had just been offered the second largest patch in the organisation next to north London.

'Think about it.'

With that he hit a buzzer, the suits reappeared and my time was up.

On the way back to my hotel my head was spinning. This was an altogether different scale. I knew Glasgow and I could get by with the rest of Scotland but London was foreign territory and not without its share of heavy hitters. In Glasgow shooters were thin on the ground. In London they grew on trees.

This was a different game on a different ground.

In my hotel room I fell back on to my bed and let my head wander. I suspected this was another offer I couldn't refuse. Martin was more than capable of running the operation in Scotland and, if I showed a lack of ambition, or worse, a lack of gratitude, I would get short shrift.

I went for a walk but I knew my time in Glasgow was up and when I got back to the hotel I made the call and said I was in.

Chapter 17

I didn't go back to Glasgow that weekend. In fact I didn't see Glasgow again for near on eighteen months. London was a cold turkey job. There was no induction. Giles pissed off to the north and I took his seat the day after my meeting at the council house.

I relied on Martin to mothball my homes back north and keep things going. I had him ship me my clothes and a few bits and pieces. When the package arrived I realised, not for the first time, that when it came down to it, I really needed very little of my worldly goods to move on.

I was based in Blackheath in an apartment not far from the grass. From day one I was Jock unless the person was face to face with me when I was Sir. I had a learning curve that made going to the moon look easy. I knew no-one, I knew little of what was going on and my reputation was worth zip.

For a fortnight I tried to get up to speed and used what charm I had to try to endear myself to the people I needed day to day. This failed in a big way. They just took the piss. The final straw came as I was unwinding over a pint in the local, three weeks to the day since I had taken over.

Giorgio, my number two - he was the one that wasn't up to the main man's job - a fourth generation Greek with a first generation accent, was leaning on me for a bigger cut or he was for the off. He knew I needed him and was striking while the iron was burning a hole in my shirt. He wanted double what he currently got and since I had the same deal in London as in Scotland this would come straight out of my pocket.

I listened and tried to reason with him but the more I talked the more it sounded like a negotiation. At one point I got up and went for a slash. The urinals were all occupied so I used a cubicle.

As I let go I heard a familiar voice enter and I listened as Mike Ashby, Giorgio's minder, gobbed off about how his pay was just about to double.

I realised that Giorgio had already pocketed the increase he was asking for. This was going nowhere good and I needed to act. I pulled the chain and exited, nodding a hello to Mike who suddenly looked like he wanted to be somewhere else. I walked up to Giorgio and said 'Let's take a walk.' He objected but I told him I needed some air to consider his position and he stood up to follow me out.

It was a clear night and we walked towards the heath talking nonsense but keeping the nonsense around Giorgio's demands and he followed like a lap dog.

We entered the heath and the street lights lost the battle with the dark. Giorgio wanted to know where we were going but, before he finished the question, I squared up to him and gave him my best Glasgow kiss – a head butt to the forehead. He went down in a heap and I lashed out with my foot and caught him in the face. Something broke and he screamed and tried to get up. I lifted my foot and brought it down on his hand and crunched half a dozen bones. He howled and, for good measure, I kicked him in the groin.

I bent down, grabbed his hair and pulled his head up.

'You're gone by tomorrow. I mean gone.'

Chapter 18

How is the clock doing? Not long. I need to speed up.

News of the incident with Giorgio spread like wildfire and I was eyed with a combination of suspicion and respect.

Giorgio left London - although to this day I have no idea where he went. I appointed a young lad called Spencer Cline as my number two. This managed to piss off about half the team I worked with, as Spencer was a new recruit I had employed on Martin's recommendation. Spencer had worked with Martin in London for a few years and I needed someone who was loyal to me and not the old school.

I dumped the nicely, nicely approach and went for the cold heartless bastard approach. I found I was good at it and kicking backsides was something I seemed to do well.

I re-organised the set up and appointed ten direct reports, each with their own remit. We met every Monday at 10.00am and Spencer was charged with taking the notes. He encrypted them and sent them out on the Tuesday. This was business and I had a target in my head – make south London number one.

This took balls. London wasn't like Glasgow. You could walk a quarter of a mile in London and be on someone else's patch. You could walk another ten yards and be in your grave. This was truly Long Good Friday land and, with one mind on how it all finished for Bob Hoskins, I had to get down and dirty.

I went after local gangs with a simple offer – join or cease to be. This led to more pitched battles than was good for a man. We fought where needed and some months we could be found knife in hand, gun in back pocket for fifteen nights straight. We rattled cages in a big way and we didn't always win. But we won enough and a year after I joined we overhauled the north as the biggest earner.

I didn't stop there. In less than eighteen months I was running out of steam south of the river. Most of the gangs that mattered were either on our side or were gone. Gaining new income was proving tougher. We set in motion some big jobs but these took time and were risky. So I turned my attention to the East End.

Technically this was north of the river but Giles was in no shape to tackle it. Unlike myself, Giles had taken a more laissez faire approach to his new job. After all it was already the biggest so why bust your nuts trying to grow it. As such he let a mean little fucker called Graham Stern go unchecked and he was now in control of most everything east of India Dock.

Graham was half German on his dad's side and couldn't have been more at home had he put on jackboots and a swastika. He was psychotic and like most psychopaths clever with it. Killing was no issue to him, as he didn't value anyone but himself and his boyfriend - a circus acrobat called Helmut that hung around him like a cheap necklace.

Being gay back then still wasn't acceptable but Graham had a wife for show and nobody messed with Graham and Helmut. If they did, they didn't do it twice.

He worked out of an old mill in Silvertown and lived in the west end. He started work at six in the morning and was rarely home before midnight. I could see the writing on the wall even if my co-workers were blind. This boy was aiming for the top but neither Giles nor the old man seemed bothered. So I decided to go head to head and take him out.

I remember the night we went in. Dark as a fat man's sphincter. The cloud cover was full and the moon new. The lighting in Silvertown was poor. The lateness of the hour was accompanied by a mist that drifted off the river and settled like a wet blanket on the roads.

There were twenty one of us. All armed and all fully aware of what we were getting into.

The operation was simple. The same old story - cut off the head of the monster and let the rest die. We concentrated everything on getting into Graham's office and hitting him hard.

At first things went well. The darkness was good cover and the mist deadened any noise we made. The entrance to the industrial estate was unguarded and Stern's office light blazed like a beacon from the third floor of the old mill. There were two guards at the entrance but they looked bored and were swigging liberally from a hip flask. By the time we landed on them they were too drunk to respond and we were in.

I hung back letting Spencer take point. We flooded up the stairs and into the office and hit trouble.

Our scout had told us there were three or four in the building but when we opened the door I counted five times that number. We had the element of surprise but not for long and instead of a quick in and out we ended up in a fire-fight while Stern fled.

I ordered Spencer and two others to follow me to chase down Stern. We left the team to slug it out and flew down the stairs to the sound of retreating gunfire. We caught the taillights of a BMW as it fishtailed out of the complex. Running for our car we gave chase but, in the mist, it was a hopeless cause and we lost them.

We cruised for an hour before heading back to Stern's office. The fire-fight was over and we had control but without Stern it was a hollow victory. We leaned on his team but they were either too scared to talk or didn't know where he was. I needed to finish this and finish it with pace.

Spencer piped up and suggested we try his home. It was a long shot but if he was going to go to ground he might try and fly by his house first. It was worth a shot.

I knew where he lived and, leaving my crew to clean up, we put metal to metal and screamed through a fog bound London.

Stern lived in a mews in the west end and by the time we got there the fog was taking on the grey of dawn. We stopped at the end of his road and I saw Stern's car, engine running and door open, sitting at the far end.

He emerged with a briefcase in one hand, a screaming woman dragging her heels in the other. She was dressed for bed and it was clear that the current Mrs Stern wasn't a happy bunny. I signalled for the others to follow me in.

I didn't care if he got in the car as there was only one way out and we had enough firepower to bring down a Panzer tank.

He saw us when we were two doors from his house, leapt into the car and gunned the engine. Without closing the car door he slammed the car into reverse, and aimed for the middle of the road.

Spencer pulled out his gun and let loose. The rear window shattered, the car slewed to one side and smashed into the front door of the house nearest to us. We waited for Stern to emerge but, apart from the engine racing in neutral, and exhaust pouring into the night there was no other action.

Spencer walked up to the car door with his gun beaded on where Stern would exit. He reached the car and looked in. He turned round to look at me and drew his hand across his throat. It was all I needed to know and we left as Mrs Stern bore down on the car in hysterics.

The next morning I received a call from Giles. He was verging on apoplectic as he screamed down the phone. I let him rant and then hung up. Ten minutes later the boss phoned and asked what the hell was going on. I told him what had happened and why. He asked me to wait by the phone.

Half an hour later a car turned up outside the office and one of the boss's bears hustled me into the back seat. We headed north to a small hotel in the village of Pangbourne on Thames. I was shown to a room at the back of the hotel and told to wait.

Ten minutes rolled by before the boss walked in.

With two bears in tow, he walked up to me and, knuckleduster in hand, cracked open my chin. I went down like a lump of clay and the bears played football with me for five minutes.

'Stop,' came the boss's voice.

The football stopped and I was dragged back onto a chair.

'Giles is out. You are in. The whole of London is yours but pull another trick like that without my permission and you'll join Karl Marx up at Highgate Cemetery.'

With this he left and, with three busted ribs, a snapped wrist and a busted jaw I took a taxi back to London - stopping off at Gerry the Fix's gaff for some emergency medical repairs.

How's the clock? Eleven thirty nine and four seconds.

So there I was kingpin in London. Top of the tree and not yet thirty. I took to the new job with a ruthless streak that earned me the nickname 'the bastard'. Unoriginal but accurate.

I was now earning more in a week than some of my old school friends would earn in a year. I kept Spencer as my number two, split London into five areas – north, south, east, west and the city - and put a body in place for each. I drove the organisation hard and turned it from an opportunistic, street-fighting mob into a sophisticated business. We embraced technology and the financial markets and turned from petty loan sharking to money, drugs and sex.

I lost four of my best men in early 1991 to a hit and run by a gang who came up from the south west with ambitions to knock me over. We repaid the favour by wiping out the entire gang. Most people will have heard of it. We crashed a turboprop with thirty people on board as it took off from Bristol airport. Sabotage was suspected but never proven.

In the summer of 1993 a money laundering scheme that had doubled our income in the previous six months went tits up in a bad way. The financial authorities sent in the heavy mob and they were the Andrews Liver Salts to our digestion. I lost six of my best men to Wormwood Scrubs for sentences ranging from three to eight years. I escaped by the skin of my teeth but my card was marked.

By now the police were wise to us in a big way but I was careful to give them little reason to talk to me. London was now over three quarters of the total income of the group and I was pushing to take control of the rest of England. I reckoned we could triple our income if I had the steering wheel.

Of course you can see what's coming. Sadly so could the boss. I was no longer a valued asset. I was becoming a serious risk to his command.

One sunny Tuesday a blue Ford Escort parked outside my townhouse in Chelsea at five in the morning and, as I left the front door two hours later, it exploded - taking out half a block of London's most expensive real estate.

I should have died but, as I left the house, I bent down to tie a shoe lace. The initial blast wave caught me in the backside and threw me into the basement well that sat beneath my front door. Out of the way of the main explosion I survived but was rendered deaf in one ear and suffered second degree burns to a fifth of my body. I had more cuts and bruises than could be counted and my Rolex was branded into my wrist. To this day I still carry the imprint of a watch on my skin.

I spent three months in hospital, all the time fearing that the boss would finish the job. But he had gotten sloppy in his old age and word was everywhere that he was behind the failed attempt on my life. He went to ground. I might have been known as 'the bastard' but at least I was a fair bastard and rule number one in our game is don't shit on your own doorstep.

Two days before I left hospital a young man called Greg McAllister took a walk in Hyde Park with his pet Labrador. It was a routine he had been repeating for a fortnight and, as he had done for the previous fourteen mornings, he uttered a polite good morning to an old man in a jogging suit flanked by two human four by twos. Only this time he took a small pistol from his coat and emptied the gun into the old man before running off.

I was now in charge of the UK and had no intention of stopping there.

Chapter 19

Sometime after I left hospital I was given a copy of Little Caesar starring Edward G Robinson to watch while I was laid up. Robinson plays Riko, probably one of the best known gangsters in movie history. I loved the movie. No – I adored the movie. Robinson became a bit of a role model. He took no shit.

There is a scene where he suspects that one of his gang is feeling guilty and about to go to confess all to the priest. Riko's solution was to gun the gang member down on the steps of the church. I must have watched that movie a hundred times and I made it clear that I no longer wanted to be known as the bastard or Jock - and soon I was the new Riko.

People thought I was off my head but I loved it.

I had just entered my fourth decade and was one of the main players in my game. Life was sweet and I set about making myself comfortable. I called Martin down from Glasgow and put him and Spencer on the day to day stuff.

I thought Martin might object. After all he had happily grown roots in Glasgow and, apart from the odd phone call, he had been a stranger. He surprised me by jumping on a train and joining me.

I muscled up with bodyguards that were smart enough to know how to defend me and thick enough to do it regardless of the danger to themselves. I bought a pile in the country and adopted the landed gentry motif with consummate ease. Shotguns, wellies, hounds and a Land Rover Defender - I was lord of the manor – in true Only Fools and Horses style. I probably looked like a tit but I didn't care - the money was rolling in and I was well smart enough to keep things on an even keel. At least I thought I was.

Eleven forty eight and twenty seven seconds – time flies when you're telling a good story.

For five years I made hay and rolled in the folding stuff for fun. I had the sense to stay out of Ireland but Wales and Scotland were mine. The north east of England held out for a while but a face to face (by face to face I mean fifty odd on each side) in South Shields and we sorted it out.

I know I wasn't the only criminal in the country. I was one of thousands but I was nearer the top of the tree than rolling in the manure at the base of the trunk.

A year later Carl Dupree rolled up at my manor. He stood on my lawn, took out a spray can and wrote in six feet letters, bright red six feet letters: 'The End.'

That's when things got weird and I mean plenty weird.

Chapter 20

The sun rose on the red lettering on my lawn as three gardeners cut out the turf and replaced it with less offensive grass. Dupree had done a runner of extraordinary speed and grace. I didn't know his name that day but I vowed to find out double quick. I ordered Martin and Spencer to the mansion and told them they had twenty four hours to find the man on the lawn and bring him to me.

They left, heads held high - the way they walked boosting my sense of well being. I would have the bastard in front of me in less than a day.

Three days rolled by and my blood pressure rose by the hour. I ranted and I raved. I screamed and I threatened. I blew a fuse, put in a new one and blew it again. All to no avail. Dupree had gone to ground and no one seemed to know who he was or where he had fled.

The lack of progress was starting to hurt. I had been dissed in my own home and I seemed powerless to act. That sort of story can gather legs and kick you in the nuts. I put thirty grand on the man's head and let it be known that whoever brought him in would also get a boot up the promotion tree.

A week later and I had attained an altogether new level of apoplexy. All other matters were thrown to the wind as I upped the ante to fifty grand and a brand new five series Beemer.

Both Martin and Spencer told me to drop it but that just made me more determined to track the painter down. I set about it with a vengeance pulling in favours that should have been left owing. I dedicated 24/7 to the hunt and left Martin and Spencer to run the business.

A month later I woke up to find the red lettering was back only this time it was more specific.

'The End. One week.'

I checked the CCTV cameras that had been installed but all I got was a grainy black and white picture of someone on the lawn at three in the morning. I had the fit to end all fits and threw everything I had at tracking the painter down.

A week sped away and seven days later I was sitting in the office when I heard a commotion down stairs. I stood up, just in time to greet an industrial quantity of police officers as they flooded into the room.

I was handcuffed and thrown in the back of a police car and taken to Paddington Green police station. It wasn't the first time this had happened but it was the most heavy-handed. I asked for my lawyer as soon as I could and was left in a holding cell until he arrived. I told him to get me out and he duly vanished to do my bidding. When, after an hour, he hadn't returned I hammered on the cell door demanding to see him again.

Twenty more minutes of sitting in the cell and he reappeared - the look on his face was not positive.

I can still remember his opening words in glorious Technicolor:

'Someone has dropped you in it. I mean SERIOUSLY dropped you in it.'

Sixteen months later I was sentenced to twenty years. The charges were as deep and wide as the Clyde. The last five years of my life were paraded in front of the court like an open book. Accounts, photographs, witness statements, copies of correspondence – you name it - it was thrown at me. It was as if someone had recorded my every thought and gesture over the last five years.

My lawyer told me that only someone on the inside could have done this. I thanked him for that particular pearl of wisdom with a smack round the head. I had figured that out ten minutes after they started the questioning.

When Martin took the witness box, under immunity from prosecution, I stood up in the court and told him he was dead. The judge held me in contempt but I was going down big style and didn't give a fuck.

Martin poured out damning evidence like a fresh torrent and by the time he finished I was so screwed my lawyer told me to try and cut a deal. I refused. It would have meant grassing up on my colleagues and even under threat of a life sentence I wasn't going to roll on people.

I entered prison on the fourth of November nineteen ninety three. I served fourteen years across five prisons and was released one year and three days ago.

By then I had lost everything. Dupree - I had by now discovered his name - moved into the patch and Martin and Spencer vanished. Some of my colleagues stayed on but most left or met messy ends.

I had only one visitor in fourteen years.

It was two years from the end of my stretch. With no one returning calls, no one visiting or no one answering letters, I had been well and truly cut off years ago.

My status in the prison was worth shit and I had received a regular stream of kickings – mainly from people I had crapped on as I had risen up the scum pond. You would think that it would have stopped as the years rolled by but there was always someone new that recognised me and took delight in reminding me of what I had done to them.

Visiting time had long since stopped being a hope and, with freedom on the horizon, I should have been in a better place but I was so depressed that I was almost revelling in my pain. When the guard told me I had a visitor I laughed at him. I hadn't had a visitor since day one. When Rachel Score walked into the visiting room I laughed again. I could fathom no reason for the visit.

She sat opposite me in a dress that was three sizes too small with five-inch stilettos that she struggled to walk in. Her face was a cake of make up and her hair a badly cropped mush. I could still see what Martin saw in her, but only just.

She never said a word. She reached into her purse and took out a battered envelope and handed it to me. Then she was gone. I rammed the envelope into my pocket before a guard could see it and, back in my cell, took it out.

I opened it and inside there was a single sheet of typed paper.

'Hi Riko,

I bet you didn't expect to hear from me. I'm sorry I had to do what I had to do but things are not quite as they seem. I've no doubt that you are planning some sort of revenge on Dupree and I don't blame you but, if I were you, I would leave it. Dupree is an evil fucker and fourteen years in prison is small change to what he could do to you if he wanted.

When you get out why don't you have a pint for old times sake. I've left one behind the bar of our old haunt. If the pub is gone by the time you get out I've asked Stevie to take care of things.

Stay safe.

Martin'

The letter is in the diary next to you.

Look at the time eleven fifty eight and forty seconds. Time to go. While I'm away, read the diary. It might help explain some things. I won't be long.

See you soon.

Diary 2008

Dear Reader

Somehow Dear Reader sounds a bit naff but it will do. What follows is a diary - of sorts. I have worked from the digital recordings that I was given. As such the following is a transcription of conversations, monologue and other assorted meanderings. It wasn't the easiest task I have ever performed and, at times some of the text may take a little license – all in the interest of keeping the whole thing lucid.

I've marked it all up in diary fashion, as the recordings frequently referred to the dates. As such it seemed logical to display it in this form.

You are probably reading this and wondering what I am gibbering on about but, hopefully, it will all make sense when you read the 'diary'.

Enjoy.

Giles Taylor

Tuesday January 1st 2008

I don't know why I'm using this thing. It has taken me a week just to work out how it operates. It's a digital recorder and I've never used one before but, after fourteen years in prison, the world is a scary place and I need some order in my life.

It's a tiny object and I've already discovered that I can keep it in my top pocket and record conversations without anybody knowing. I'm intending to keep an 'aural' record of the next few months – if I can work the bloody thing.

I was given it on Christmas day by the hostel and told it might help if I use it to note down my thoughts. It had been left by a well wisher and, as the new boy, I was trusted to use it and not hock it for drink money. I think the idea is a pile of crap but in a world of iPods, broadband, HD TV and SEO I'm like a polar bear in the Sahara – wrong place and lost.

I have a hangover - my first New Year hangover in nearly a decade and a half. A couple of the lads at the hostel managed to blag a few bottles of Buckfast and a half bottle of Glen's, and we celebrated the birth of 2008.

I'm stunned at how little I have in the world. That bastard Dupree took everything. He owns my homes; he raided my bank accounts and even emptied my offshore account. When I stepped out of the prison gates I had the clothes I stood in and one hundred and eight quid in my pocket (the money I had on me when I was arrested).

I was given a bed in a hostel near Hammersmith for two weeks. Two weeks that I spent trying to get back on the ladder that I had fallen from - but it would seem that Dupree has ensured that the first rung is so out of sight that I may as well try and climb Mount Everest in a pair of slippers.

I door-stepped those of the gang who were still around and got blanked. I tried those who had retired but was told my name was bad news. I received eight kickings in as many days and the writing was on the wall. London was not for me. I was so skint I had to hold up a local corner store to get enough cash for a ticket back home.

Glasgow was little better. Everyone is drawing me a blank but the kicking ratio has fallen – only three so far.

I'm sitting on the edge of a single bed in a room that sleeps four. My room mates are all out looking for booze. It's what they do every night. I'm not there yet but a few more weeks and I might take to the slippery slope with gusto.

Rachel's letter is stuffed into my holdall. I've read it so often I can tell you the spacing between letters in millimetres and could, if asked, forge it to the point where a handwriting expert would struggle to tell original from copy.

I'm planning a trip to the pub tomorrow. I've no idea if it is still there or if Stevie is to be found. Not that I have a blind clue as to who Stevie is.

My head hurts and I'm off to the front desk for some painkillers.

Wednesday January 2nd 2008

The trip to the pub was a washout. The Lame Duck is no more. A concrete shell with a faded wooden sign that some local wit has changed to The Lame Fuck. There was no sign of life and no indication of who owns it and how you could contact them. I tried a few of the nearby pubs but it was early and the bar staff were clueless – mostly telling me to come back later when the owner or manager was around.

I took myself up to the West End for a memory trip but I wasn't in the mood. Everything reminds me of what I used to have. If it wasn't the New Year break I would have ended up sitting in Victoria Park mixing with the retired, unemployed and scum – sad to say that today I was probably the only one that could lay claim to all three categories. The whole world was out taking the air - trying to shake off the excesses of the New Year and it made me feel crap.

I ate a Kit Kat but I wasn't in need of the break – my life is one big break. Maybe tomorrow I'll try the council and find out who used to hold the license at The Lame Duck.

Friday January 4th 2008

I spent yesterday in the hostel. It might have been a Thursday, a work day, and the other side of the traditional two day New Year break in Scotland but that didn't mean that the people I needed to see in the council were back to work. Monday I was told on the phone. It cost me twenty pence to find that out. I don't have twenty pence to spare – how bad are things when you can't afford to make a 20p phone call.

One of my roommates - Charles - or 'the Stink' as he is affectionately known - and I use the term 'affectionately' in the loosest possible sense - told me to try the web.

I blanked this idea. I'm ashamed to say I must be the least web literate person in the UK. For most of my time in prison there was no internet access – the web revolution passed us all by. When they did install it, we were restricted in where we could surf and I just couldn't be arsed. I did try to Google Dupree once but to no avail and never went back.

There is an internet terminal in the hostel and I've asked one of the kids if they can find out who the owner of The Lame Duck is but he wants a packet of fags for his trouble so I told him to piss off.

I'll wait until Monday and do the physical thing and visit the council.

Saturday January 5th 2008

A bad night last night. I went for a walk about eight o'clock to clear my head. I met a few of my inmates on the steps of the hostel and they were off to get slammed up in the Necroplolis – the soon to be dead drinking with the long dead. I declined. Things are bad but not that bad - 'the Stink' offered me a bottle of meths two nights ago and the smell alone made me gag. I'm determined to avoid that path but something in the back of my head tells me that all paths lead that way.

The hostel sits just off High St in a run down part of the city. Back in the eighteenth century this was the centre of Glasgow and the area just across the road from where I sleep is known as Merchant City - harking back to a day when the city was king of the trading towns. I'm not a kick in the arse away from where I first met Mr Read. They say what goes around comes around.

On the other side of the hostel is the 'Barras' – Glasgow's perennial market – 'If you can't get it there – you can't get it anywhere' - a direct quote from my old man. I decided to wander through the ramshackle maze of buildings that make up the market – all closed up for the night. On the edges a few pubs ply their trade but last night it was hard to imagine the buzz that the area creates when it is in full flow.

As a kid I loved coming here. The men on the stalls selling crockery at prices that seemed unreal. The smell of cooked sausage smothered in tomato sauce. The sound of music through tinny speakers hung to an outside wall by a length of clothes line.

There was a magic in the place that seemed to vanish as I got older. Did the place just get seedier or did the cynicism that comes with old age just see the place for what it really was?

I had stopped for a fag, one I had been saving since tea time, next to one of the buildings that hosts the stalls. The shutters were down all around and the street outside was deserted save for the rubbish that the wind was playing football with.

I heard them before I saw them. The thumping bass beat of dance music echoing from the windows and walls around me. There were six of them. All hooded up and all on a mission. I was clearly the target from the get go. They had no fear – music racked up - inviting attention. I'd been that boy and knew what was coming, so I dropped the cigarette and moved away.

Three more appeared at the other end of the street and I was caught in a classic pincer. I looked around for a way to escape but there was nowhere to go.

Twenty five years ago I would have known these boys and they would have known me. Now I was no more than a jakey ripe for a beating. I tried to talk to them but the hoody with the beat box simply racked up the volume. This wasn't a time for a chat – it was a time to get down and dirty on the tramp.

I didn't take the beating lying down. I can still handle myself when the need is on but sheer numbers were against me. Even so I surprised the first three by decking them and decking them hard. It caused the others to pause and reassess their strategy but numbers and booze-filled bloodstreams gave them brave pills, and they laid into me.

I curled into a ball and tried to focus on when it would be over.

The three I had laid out came to, joined in and, if it hadn't been for the distant wail of a police siren, I suspect I might have been joining my mates in the Necropolis as a more permanent member of the area.

I lay for ten minutes after the assault squad ran off and assessed the damage. I'd had enough kickings in my time to realise that a few bones had been broken. My ribs hurt and my left hand was limp – one of the bastards had dropped from a full six feet and crushed my wrist between his knee and the ground. I staggered to my feet and headed for the Royal Infirmary. It was less than a mile away but it still took me an hour to get there. Mostly because I needed to stop to hack up blood.

They kept me in overnight, strapped my ribs and put a plaster on my wrist. I had a restless night but it was free of the smell of 'the Stink' and breakfast in the morning was hot and free.

The hospital wanted me to report the attack to the police but I declined. I might have been gone for a couple of decades but there will still be some police who remember me from days gone by and I want to stay out of their way until I figure the Lame Duck/Stevie thing out.

I was discharged with a supply of painkillers and an appointment to come back in a week.

The strange thing about the whole affair was not the beating. I'm more intrigued by the fact they knew my name.

Monday January 7th 2008

Stevie is in sight. I worked my way through the black hole that is local authority bureaucracy and discovered that the licensee for The Lame Duck was one Stephen Mailer. He may or may not be the owner but there was an address for him and I scraped enough to jump a bus and pay a visit.

He lives in Bishopbriggs on the north of the City. It is a real two day camel ride by bus and when I got there he wasn't in. His home is a terraced house that doesn't suggest he is a pub entrepreneur of note. I hung around for an hour or so but to no avail.

I decided to try again in the early evening in case he was working - so I duly stretched a cup of coffee to breaking point in the nearby ASDA and went for a walk - in the main to take my mind off the fact that I had no money for food.

Around seven I headed back to Stevie's house but it still showed no signs of life. I thought about leaving a note but decided against it. The beating has sparked up my warning radar.

I headed back to the hostel and got the young internet geek to find me Stevie's phone number on the web. This was done for free – no cigarettes – just the threat of bodily violence.

Thursday January 10th 2008

So Stevie exists, is alive and well and running a pub in the nether regions of Easterhouse. I phoned him two days ago and he agreed to meet in town. I suggested the Mitchell Library – to avoid the embarrassment of meeting in a pub or café and not having the cash to buy a drink.

I'm not big on libraries. My reading tends to be The Sun and the Daily Record and if I'm in the mood for intelligent debate I dip into the Herald. I've probably read six books in my entire life and most of them were forced down my throat at school. As such the 'Mitchell' was a bit of a wonder to me.

I waited for Stevie in the old section – a grand Victorian affair that was built when libraries were almost places of worship. High vaulted ceilings, grandiose frontage and an entrance to grace a palace.

Stevie arrived bang on time. A tall slim man with hair that looked like it had gone by the time he was thirty. He wore a pair of battered jeans and a sweat top with the words Strathclyde University emblazoned across the front. It looked old. A university degree and he was a career puller of pints. That doesn't make him a bad person but university was a whole world away from my upbringing and I always envisaged it churning out the future leaders of the free world - people who rarely say – 'Will that be all?' after each sentence.

We found a table and slumped into two hard back chairs. His eyes were red. Drugs or lack of sleep – take your pick?

I opened up by handing him Martin's letter. He looked at it suspiciously. As would I given its state after all these years. He read it with care and then handed it back to me.

'I haven't seen Martin since Christ left Govan.'

I nodded, waiting for him to open up a little but he stayed quiet.

I asked if he knew why I'd been left a pint. It sounded dumb.

'It's got fuck all to do with a pint. I wanted nothing to do with it back then. But they threatened to do some damage to my mum. Can you believe that – MY MUM. So I agreed. Take this and I'm off.'

'Who are they?'

He blanked the question and reached into his pocket, pulled out a key, dropped it on the table and was up and off before I could speak. I grabbed the key and chased him out of the building but he broke into a run, sprinted to the roadside, leapt into an old VW Beetle, locked the doors and blanked me as he pulled away.

I watched the car merge into the traffic and when I lost sight of it I opened my hand to look at the key. It was a small brass Yale type with a few serial numbers on one side. Other than that it had nothing to indicate what it was a key for.

One mystery after another but on this occasion I know someone else that might be able to help.

Friday January 11th 2008

Back to the old haunts is the order of the day. I hardly recognised the Gorbals. New flats, leisure centre and a distinct lack of many of the pubs I had frequented. I doubted that the person I wanted would still be in the same house. I doubted they would still be alive. But they were both.

The man who answered the door was bald (where he had once had a shock of ginger hair), wrinkled (where he had once had a face so smooth he had been nicknamed 'baby') and a stoop (where once he had stood tall and proud - five years in Her Majesties Armed Forces would do that to a man). Recognition flickered in his eyes and he stepped back to let me in. There was no fear – once there would have been – but my story was well kent and I was no longer a threat.

The flat was minimalist and dominated by a wretched stained coffee table that had the Mount Etna of fag ash and doots as its centre-piece. The heating was all the way up to eleven and the place smelled like nothing I had ever encountered.

There was no offer of a seat. My host collapsed in the only chair in the room. It sat square in front of the TV, next to the fag mountain and, before his backside hit the fake leather, he lit up.

'How you doing Ron?' I asked.

'Better than you from what I hear.'

That hurt. The house was a shit-hole and yet I was the one on my uppers. Go figure.

'I need a favour?'

'It will cost.'

I knew it would. I had cleaned out the geek kid for everything he had and bought forty fags. I dropped them next to the mountain.

'Small favour,' he said looking at the two packets with contempt.

I dropped the key on the table.

'What's it for?'

In the good old days Ron had been a locksmith and a bloody good one at that. In my house breaking phase Ron had been a saviour on many an occasion. It was easier to get into a house with a key and it was often surprisingly easy to snatch a key, copy it and return it to the owner. Ron did the copying for a fee at odds with the going rate on the High St, but the stiff cost paid for his silence.

He looked at the key and picked up one of the packets of cigarettes, muttering something about the wrong brand before pulling a stick from the pack and lighting up. The one in his mouth wasn't even half dead.

'Well?'

He inhaled and held up the key, twirling it over a couple of times before dropping it back on the table. He said nothing and exhaled.

'Well?'

'Safety deposit.'

'What bank?'

He inhaled again and I was seconds from landing one on him. It was like drawing teeth from a crocodile.

I waited.

'Can't be sure.'

He drew on the cigarette again and I changed tack. Stepping behind him I wrapped my arm round his neck and pulled upward. He spat out the fag and began to struggle but he was old and I had a fourteen year stretch of using the prison gym in my arms.

'Be sure,' I said.

His choking was getting in the way of his ability to talk and I loosened off a little.

'Ok, ok, no need for the heavy stuff.'

I let go but stayed behind him, ready to grab him if he made a move that looked out of place. I was staring down on his bald pate. The collection of liver spots and scabs made for an unpleasant vista.

'It ain't a bank key. This is either a Credit Union or a private box.'

'Go on.'

'There are very few private box places left. No money in them anymore. I'd put money on a Credit Union but not a new one. The key's old. Twenty years, maybe more. They don't make these anymore. Is the key local?'

'I don't know.'

'Assume it is. If we don't you're screwed. I only know three Credit Unions that might, and I mean might, still have old safety deposit boxes.'

'What's a Credit Union?'

I felt stupid asking but it was a hole in my education.

'A kind of community bank. It's run by locals and lends small amounts of money at decent rates and allows local people to save money without having to go to the bank. They also do stuff like pay your bills for you, arrange insurance and so on. There used to be lots of them when times were bad. They seem to be coming back into fashion in some areas. I'm surprised you've never heard of them given your career.'

He was referring to my loan sharking days and to be fair I was surprised at my ignorance. Maybe there had never been any on my patch?

'Where are they?'

'There's still a shed load of them around but there are only three that would have boxes for this key. There is one over in Easterhouse. One up in Castlemilk and one over in Drumchapel.'

It figures. Easterhouse, Castlemilk and Drumchapel were (along with Pollok) Glasgow's 'townships' built in the sixties.

Overcrowding was becoming a real issue for Glasgow in the fifties and the council targeted some twenty nine districts for renewal or demolition. Close on a hundred thousand homes met the wrecking ball and many of the inhabitants were shipped out to the new build 'townships' on the edge of the city. At the time it was hailed as a master stroke. In truth Glasgow lost its heart and soul, as row after row of tenements were flattened.

The planners also gave little thought to infrastructure. Thousands of people found themselves crammed into housing with few facilities. Castlemilk with a population of close on fifty thousand didn't get a pub until the early eighties – thirty years after the first house went up.

All four areas became hotbeds for gangs and trouble but now there were third world debt levels of cash being invested to rid the city of that legacy.

'If I turn up with a key will they let me use it?'

'No. You need the chit that came with the key or proof of ownership. They won't use the boxes that much now. They are not stupid. They may even have trashed them although I doubt it'

'Shit.'

I got him to write down as much as he knew about each Credit Union and left.

As I walked back to the hostel it occurred to me that I might just be about to get back into the 'breaking and entering' market again.

To do that I need to tool up.

Sunday January 13th 2008

That fuckwit Ron talked. I should have guessed. I was on the hostel steps yacking to 'the Stink' when a black Ford Mondeo cruised passed. Not unusual but when it circled for the fourth time it caught my attention. It was too early for a gang on a 'beat a tramp' trip so I just sat and talked, with one eye looking out for the Mondeo. When it slid by for the fifth time I told 'the Stink' I was going in for a cup of tea and he nodded.

Once inside I pulled up a chair near one of the front windows and sipped the monkey brew as I scanned for the Mondeo but it didn't reappear. My wrist was giving me gip and my ribs were joining in the fun. The last thing I needed was some more aggro.

Around six o'clock I went out for a walk and a think. I needed some tools of the trade but I was skint. I was just wondering if Ron still kept a spare kit when the Mondeo screamed around the corner and the doors flew open.

I didn't wait to see who was emerging and turned and ran. I hit High St with a full turn of speed and crossed the road to the wail of a horn as a bus slammed on its brakes to avoid me. As I made the pavement on the far side I looked round and saw two figures hot on my tail. Behind them the Mondeo had started moving towards me.

I headed into the Merchant City with no idea of where I was going to end up. All I knew was that I was a target and the beating the other night might be the start of something quite nasty. I hauled my backside onto Albion St and headed north.

You can only keep running flat out for a short time and I was already down to a jog. Add to that the cast on my wrist and I was struggling. Fortunately so were my pursuers.

I crossed Ingram St and kept on up Albion St and passed the old Glasgow Daily News building. I was entering Strathclyde University land and, as I ran out onto George St, I turned left and headed for George Square. I needed people around me. I was less likely to take a kicking in a public place.

I looked back. The pursuers were at the corner of Albion St and were getting into the Mondeo. I slowed to a walk. George St was one way against them and I walked out into the square, heaving breath, but safe for the moment.

The town was coming off the back of rush hour and there were still a fair number of people doing the 'going home' thing. I dropped into one of the benches that ring the western end of the square and tried to blend in while keeping a sharp lookout for the Mondeo.

It appeared five minutes later and I hunkered down as it drove by less than twenty feet away. It turned right to circle the square. I got up and headed away from it and down towards the river.

Walking down Queen St I turned onto Royal Exchange Square and then down onto Buchanan St - thank you Glasgow council for the foresight in introducing pedestrian only zones.

Every few steps I looked back expecting to see the pursuers but if they were there they were doing their best Ninja trick and keeping out of view.

As I walked I considered my options. The hostel was out. I had no idea who these jokers were but they knew where I lived and it wouldn't take a genius to stake out the hostel and wait for me. I had no one I could turn to. My return to Glasgow had been as close to a secret as I could have made it. Ron seemed an obvious mouth to have yacked.

It occurred to me that there might be another reason. The gang of boys that had beat up on me had used my name a few times and maybe the Mondeo gang and the beating weren't unconnected.

I passed the subway entrance at St Enoch's Square but dismissed it as an escape route – even if I had wanted to I didn't have the money for the ride.

I crossed over Clyde St and stepped onto the river walk that runs along the north bank of the River Clyde. To my left was a suspension bridge for pedestrians that had a claim to fame as the setting for some of the movie Gorky Park – it would seem that Moscow and Glasgow look similar in some lights. I turned away from it and headed down river, ducking as the walkway ran under one of the many bridges that cross the Clyde.

On the other side I began to walk slowly, watching the brown carpet of water slide along beside me. There was no sign of activity on the river. This far up, there never is. In the Clyde's hey day it was entirely possible to cross the river at this point by jumping from ship to ship. Now you were lucky if you saw a duck paddling.

On the far side of the river some kids were trying to hit a plank of wood floating mid stream with stones. I watched them for a while wondering at where those days had gone: the carefree afternoons when the riverbank transformed itself into one giant playground. The smallest of the kids let rip with his right arm and scored a bull's eye on the plank. A shout went up and he high fived thin air for thirty seconds.

The tallest spotted me watching them and flicked me a V before shouting something that was lost on the wind.

I think it rhymed with anchor?

I reached the Kingston Bridge - a giant concrete structure that stretches sixty or seventy feet above the river. I read once it was Europe's busiest bridge and the endless roar of tyre on asphalt did nothing to dispel the belief.

The bridge is a single span between two mighty piers. On my side a sign telling me that Her Majesty the Queen Mother had opened the bridge on June 26th 1970 was embedded in the concrete. I was wondering what I was doing on that day when I heard the slam of a door and turned to see the Mondeo less than ten yards away and the two goons launching themselves in my direction.

There are some things in life that you do that, on reflection, were both genius and insanely stupid in the same breath. This was one of those moments. I looked up and down the walkway but it was empty. I could run but there was nowhere to go. The goons would be on me in seconds and I knew this was not a good news event.

I flipped a mental coin and when the coin dropped I sprinted for the fence that stops the innocent falling into the river. In an instant I grabbed the handrail with my good hand, vaulted over and began the plunge towards the dank water.

The drop was a good twenty feet and I landed arse first and sank. My clothes combined with the cast began soaking up the river and my descent refused to reverse. I thrashed my arms around to try and pull me back to the surface. Somewhere deep down I realised that I was making things worse and my survival instinct took over. With a kick of both feet and tug of my good arm I headed up. When I broke the surface I hauled in air like a stranded whale.

I looked up at the bank and I was already fifty yards downstream. The dark waters were far from still when you were in them. I could see the goons looking at me. They had no idea what to do next and began to slowly walk down the river keeping pace with me.

The water was cold and I'm not a strong swimmer. I knew I needed to get out and I struck out for the south bank. As soon as I did this the current picked up as I crossed into the faster flowing centre of the river. A quick look back and the goons were jogging to keep up. Ahead of me was the so-called Squinty Bridge – one of Glasgow's newer river crossings. I needed to make the bank as quickly as possible or the goons would cross over and be waiting for me when I emerged.

The water was foul. The Clyde might be a million times cleaner than it was fifty years ago but it is still a country mile from being drinkable. I spat out a mouthful and knew I would need industrial strength mouthwash for a month to get rid of the taste.

The cold was starting to bite and I seemed no nearer the far bank. I looked back but the goons were out of sight.

Seconds later I was swept under the bridge. I needed to get out and even if the pursuers were waiting for me I was losing the battle with the water and a kicking was marginally better than a drowning. I had no choice but to claw my way to the bank and hope for the best.

Around me the river was hemmed in by a brick wall with a set of steel runged ladders every couple of hundred yards. Even at high tide there is still a clear ten feet between the river and the safety rails that run next to the walkway. At the moment that was closer to fifteen feet.

The next set of rungs were coming up fast and I pushed hard towards them. I wasn't sure I had the strength to keep afloat much longer.

I was close to the bank and if the goons were above me they were lost to view as the wall loomed up. The next set of rungs were twenty feet down river and I was now skimming the wall, my good hand sliding along the slime that coated everything.

I rushed towards the ladder.

The rungs were old and pitted and the lower ones were covered in the slime. As I drew level I grabbed with my good hand but it slid free. I threw my bad hand over the bottom rung and jammed my elbow into the gap between metal and wall. I screamed at the pain as it stopped my downward travel. I could feel the pressure building on my elbow joint as the river tried to drag me away from safety.

Working against the current I pulled myself a few precious inches closer to the ladder and launched myself at the next rung up. I jammed my good arm in the gap between rung and wall and then let my weight fall on it as I heaved in air. I needed to get my feet out of the water but a combination of the river's current and the way my arm was wedged tight had me with my back to the wall.

I took a deep breath and let go with my right arm and swung it high, grabbing for the next rung. At the same time I pulled hard on my left arm and felt water slide from my feet as they came free of the water. Every sinew in my body told me to let go as my wrist – already broken in several places cracked. My feet flailed around to find a foothold and I slammed my left foot onto a rung and clung on.

Ten breaths later and I straightened myself and started to climb. My clothes had tripled in weight and the cold and exertion of the swim was draining the last of my reserves. I reached the top rung and, as I placed my good hand on the top rail, a face appeared above me and my heart sank.

'Not a nice evening for a swim, sir.'

I have never, and I mean have never, been so glad to see a policeman's uniform.

Wednesday January 16th 2008

Just out of hospital and I can still taste the Clyde. I am on a course of antibiotics that would protect an army in Zaire. The doctor said it was precautionary. Given the shit in my mouth I reckon it is a fucking necessity.

The police were hardly fazed by my dip. Once I told them where I stayed, they assumed I was on drinks, drugs or both. Thankfully there was no deep questioning and neither of them recognised me.

There was no sign of the goons when I got out and I spent most of the time in the hospital planning a slow, and painful end to Ron's life. At the moment my favourite is skinning alive and dipping in a tub of salt but I think I can do better. But the truth is I'm not sure it was him that grassed me up. Not sure at all.

The Credit Unions are next on my to do list. I need to go back into the breaking and entering business and that requires some serious planning.

If I'm right about the goons and the kickings then someone has it in for me and I suspect that the key is all part of it – but I may be wrong.

I'll have to case all three Credit Unions and suss out the best way in. Priority one is a new toolkit. One that allows for contingencies. The days of a stethoscope and sandpaper for your finger tips may be long gone but a decent toolkit will still suffice for most needs. The only problem with that is the price tag. I need cash and then I need to find a source for the kit.

Cash first.

My options are as follows:

Mugging – but I'm out of practice and anyway some of the people you think are fat, lazy or defenceless aren't, and some people are just penniless. Anyway who can go mugging with a buggered wrist? So that's out.

A little bit of armed robbery – pick a corner store and a weapon and we are away. Problem is I don't have a weapon and you really need a gun to do a shop job justice. A gun will cost more than a tool kit – so that's out.

Housebreaking – a racing favourite at the moment. Back to school for me. The right house and I can purchase a small lock pick kit and it's time to roll.

Friday January 18th 2008

I have acquired a small lock pick kit with no need to return to burglary.

My luck might be changing.

The computer geek put me onto it. There is a small lost property cupboard at the back of the building. It rarely has anything in it. Those that have little rarely lose things – and none of my fellow inmates have more than a penny between them. However, on the odd occasion a new boy rolls up and, fearing for his possessions, asks the staff to look after them. They use the lost property cupboard as a safe place to store stuff. The guests soon discover that their belongings are a dam sight safer under their bed than under the watchful eye of the staff.

Not that the staff are dishonest but they are careless.

The geek told me that a new boy had checked in. As was my wont I ignored him until he also informed me that the new boy was an ex con called Sid Montgomery.

Now I know a Sid Montgomery of old. Not by sight but by reputation. He was a burglar much in the same mould as myself only he worked the Solway coast. He had a good rep and a fondness for hard liquor. More than once he had been caught in someone's house; passed out with the contents of the owner's drinks cabinet in his stomach.

I did a bit of asking and it transpired that the Sid I knew and Sid the new boy were one and the same.

It wasn't the greatest piece of Sherlockian deduction to figure he might be holding a kit on his person or in his bag.

Fortunately he had decided to hand in his bag and the staff duly placed it in the lost property cupboard, as it was the only place with a lock. A paperclip took care of the lock and a quick rifle of Sid's bag revealed a small but adequate tool kit. I pocketed it, returned his bag to the cupboard and locked it.

I took the kit to the rear of the hotel and, placing it in a plastic bag, buried it in the flower bed. If Sid reported the kit missing they would turn the place upside down looking for it.

Sometimes it feels like I simply swapped one prison for another. The lack of bars and guards seems to matter little. In my head I feel as trapped as ever.

In my fourteen years as a guest of Her Majesty I had dreamed of the moment that I would walk free the way a teenager dreams of his first sexual encounter. Now I was out there seems to be no freedom in my freedom. An ex con, no cash, living in a hostel – at least back in prison I had hope. Out here hope should be piled high around every corner. I just don't seem to be finding the right corners at the moment but maybe Sid's lockpick is a start.

I'm off to case the Easterhouse Credit Union tomorrow.

Sunday January 20th 2008

I forgot it was Saturday. I lose track so easily. It was after lunch before I got there and it was closed.

The building sits in a row of shops in a run down mall. The mall is the epitome of a shopping experience in one of Glasgow's more challenged areas. In order, left to right as you look at them from the pavement - the row of shops contains the following - Charlies - fish and chips, Ho Wah - Chinese take away, Five in One - kebabs et al, Mother India - Indian, Tantastic - sun beds for the masses, 'Booze for All' - cheap drink, Kenny's - sweets and fags, Easterhouse Credit Union, Priced Out - corner store, MacWilliams - bookies.

It doesn't take much of a challenge to the intellect to realise why some areas of Glasgow have a life expectancy twenty years less than others.

The whole block is a sixties strip with a car park on the roof. Behind it lies a small lane that provides access for deliveries. A couple of CCTV cameras pay lip service to security but the real issue is the out and out quantity of plate steel that rolls down of a night and protects the front and back of the shops.

The shop owners are no fools and the Credit Union is no exception. I'm not sure what I had in my head but my target isn't welcoming me with open arms. The shutter is a serious deterrent and the locks that bind it to the pavement would need plastic explosive to break them.

The rear is not much better but, as with every break-in I've ever been involved in, the obvious routes are always the best and the most obvious is the tiny window that sits next to the back door.

Unlike the door it is protected by a wire grill not a steel shutter, but it is sturdy and the window is re-enforced mesh glass. It looks too small to let a man through but you would be amazed at what you can slip through if you have to.

Tomorrow I'll suss out the other two and then it's down to the hard bit.

Monday January 21st 2008

I've hit a slight problem. Although the Castlemilk Credit Union is a doddle, it's almost a mirror of the one in Easterhouse and, better still, the window at the back has no grill, relying instead on the wire mesh that runs through the small pane - Drumchapel is a different kettle of fish altogether.

For a start it is inside a new shopping mall with all the attendant security that that now entails. It sits near the south entrance but when the mall is locked down it's patrolled by security guards and is heaven for CCTV junkies – there has to be a couple of dozen that I saw and I probably missed half. To make matters worse the Credit Union has a steel shutter and there is no rear access to the shop.

I'll start with Castlemilk and if it's a blank I'll try Easterhouse. If I'm still none the wiser to the key's secret I'll need to figure a way to crack Drumchapel.

Castlemilk is on for tonight.

Tuesday January 22nd 2008

A dud and a bad dud at that. I arrived at the row of shops in Castlemilk after 11.00pm and almost got myself in a fight straightaway as I stumbled on a gang of lads glugging MD 20/20 in the lane behind. Four or five bottles to the good and the six of them were up the far end of the lane.

At first, I thought I could break in and leave them be but, as I walked down the lane, I was spotted and they started towards me. I did the manful thing and retreated, waiting for half an hour before I chanced my arm again.

This time they were sitting outside the Credit Union back door and starting to kick up some nonsense. One of them was balancing on the wall that bordered the lane and was trying to back-flip like a beam gymnast. It was never going to end well and he crashed to the ground to the amusement of his mates.

I watched them fanny around for twenty minutes and when they cracked open another bottle I considered walking away but, just then, I heard footsteps behind me. Before I could move I was slammed into the wall as ten or twelve boys hurtled past screaming and shouting. The next I knew, there was the battle of Bannockburn going on in the lane and, by the sounds of things, the new gang were no less the worse for wear on the alcohol front than the gang they were attacking.

I watched from the relative safety of the end of the lane as the fight geared up. Ten minutes in and the police siren on the wind told me someone had dialled 999. I turned, sprinted across the road, dived into a close in the tenement opposite and waited for the police to arrive.

Three patrol cars cruised up to the entrance of the lane – blues and twos now in quiet mode. They pulled up out of sight of the lane and seven policemen got out. There was the faint buzz of a radio and then they disappeared around the corner and into the lane. Seconds later bodies started streaming out of the lane entrance. The police emerged a few minutes later with five of the boys in tow. They were thrown into the back of the cars and it was over before it really had a chance to begin.

I heard a door open behind me and turned to see a figure emerging from the dark.

'Whit the fuck are you doing?'

The voice sounded heavy with drink. Does every fucker drink round here?

'Just avoiding the nonsense out there,' I said, pointing to the entrance of the close.

'I don't give a shit. Piss off or I'll break your legs.'

Outside the police were still tidying up and I needed to be part of that scene like a hole in the head.

'I'll be out of your hair in two minutes.'

The stranger was now in sight, lit by the glow of the streetlights from outside and oozed wee man syndrome in a big way. I've seen it all before - men shorter than they want to be, making up for it by being aggressive unreasonable shits. Trying to add inches to their height by acting the big man. It stinks and can be a pain in the arse but I was fucked if I was going to let some little shit with a vertical complex piss on me.

He had brave pills going on and stepped in close. I could smell the booze as the vapour wafted up my nose - his head barely up to my shoulder.

'You'll be out of my hair right fuckin' now.'

I turned to him and, as the car doors were still shutting behind me, I lifted my right knee, grabbed his mouth with my good hand and sunk a knee deep into his bollocks. My hand caught the scream. I pushed his head back and caught his leg with my foot and sent him to the ground.

Dropping to my knees I grabbed his head and slammed it onto the concrete with as much force as I could muster. His head bounced and he groaned. I balled my fist and slammed it into his gut and stood up. He wasn't out cold but he was well fucking gubbed. I looked out of the close and was rewarded with the sight of retreating tail lights. I gave one glance at the stranger and exited. It was good to know I could still handle myself if needed. Even if it was against a midget drunk.

I crossed the road and entered the lane with no thought that my victim would be after me. I was sure the wee man would gather himself up and head home. Calling the police would be the last thing on his mind.

I reached the back door of the Credit Union, took out a small torch from my pocket and played it around the edge of the window. I was looking for the tell tale shadow of a tremble alarm but if it was there it was well hidden. That was a surprise. I had expected a tougher gig than this. After all this was all but a bank in name.

I took out a curled up piece of cloth from under my jacket and laid it on the ground. I unfurled it and, in the half light, selected a ball and preen hammer along with a small punch. I placed the point of the punch at the bottom left corner of the mesh window and struck it with the hammer.

The punch went through and the glass spidered. I repeated the operation until the bottom corner was a maze of cracks. I turned the hammer over, using the preen to finish driving a hole in the corner.

Grabbing the busted glass I levered it away from the window. Putting some welly into it I pulled again and the rest of the window peeled away like Blu-Tac on a warm day. I forced the window to bend up into the top right corner. The mesh held the glass together and the whole window now hung from the frame like a bent and twisted shutter.

I cleared away the sharp edges around the frame with the hammer and shone the small torch into the room beyond. It was stacked full with boxes and in one corner there was a small table with a wooden chair in attendance. High up in the top corner was a small white box. An infrared passive detector.

In my day such technology was the domain of the rich and powerful. Nowadays it was available from Tesco's and would almost certainly be linked to the local police station. I wasn't worried. I had no intention of being inside for more than a few minutes.

I had spent the last few days getting to know the layout of all three jobs in intimate detail. As my cell mate for the first four years inside had said to me on more occasions than I cared to remember – planning is everything. The fact he had been caught during an opportunistic house breaking seemed to pass him by.

Beyond the room was the main shop - an open area that served the public. No counters. No wire cages. Open plan was the order of the day and the safe was in the room next to this one. A bottle of Glen's vodka, that I could ill afford, and a long term customer that I had befriended in the local pub had given me the low down – to the smallest detail. She had once worked there and knew the layout inside out. Yes, she had told me, there were some safety deposit boxes but only half a dozen and they were rarely used. She didn't know if there were any that hadn't been touched in years but she told me she wouldn't be surprised.

All I had to do was exit the door from the room I was looking at, turn left, enter the next one and I was in the safe room. My friend had assured me that the door to the safe room wasn't strengthened and the plan was simple – in and out as quickly as possible.

I pulled up my hood, heaved myself onto the window and, as I slid through the gap, the red light blinked and the alarm went off. I rolled on the floor and, kicking boxes out of the way, I rushed through the door and into the shop.

But my friendly snitch had either lied or was out of date with her info. The other door was locked and it was a heavyweight son of a bitch. I'd had visions of kicking the thing in but given the CCTV cameras

I hadn't dared enter the building to check it myself. Mistake. It took me ten minutes to crack the lock and I knew that the police were on their way but the fact they had just lifted five of the gang gave me hope that they might be light on back up.

The ten minutes seemed like ten hundred and my ears were only listening for one sound - sirens.

The door opened and I pushed inside to find a mother of a safe door on the right and a dozen boxes on the left. I whipped out the key and in sixty seconds knew that I had drawn a blank. I exited, head down to the camera and I was back in the lane in less than a minute. The sirens were on the rise again but I vanished into the scheme before the police could arrive.

Tonight it's Easterhouse.

Wednesday January 23rd 2008

Dud number two. Much easier than Castlemilk though. I knew the boxes were in the room I was breaking into and the wire mesh on the window was a breeze to cut through. I was in and out in two minutes and back in the hostel by one o'clock.

Now things get tricky. Drumchapel is a bastard. I've been over there four times and I'm still clueless. In the old days I would just have walked in with a couple of gorillas and concluded my business. With no back up and no weapon it's a non-starter. They will also be on high alert. Word will have spread that someone is doing Credit Unions. That will make them twitchy. I need some help on this one and sadly I can only think of one person that might be up for it.

I'm off to see Martin tomorrow.

God help me.

Thursday January 24th 2008

For the bulk of my incarceration I had always thought that Dupree had taken Martin out after I was sent down. Then I had the pleasure of a new cell mate, a confidence trickster, who shared my cell for a few nights. It meant there were three of us crammed in the room built for one but the prison was bursting at the seams and there was hardly a union rep we could complain to.

The con was called Gerald Crainey and in some distant part of my brain his name rang a bell. At first he said little but on the third night we were talking football and he came over all gobby. It turned out he had been on the books for Celtic as a schoolboy.

'I could have played for the first team, you know.'

He loved his football and to hack him off I told him I was a Partick Thistle fan. He took the royal piss out of me but we got into it over the 1971 game and, as I had learned over the years, it was a great way to wind up some Celtic fans.

'Another Partick nutter. Met one not long ago called Martin Sketchmore.'

I backed him up and asked him if Martin Sketchmore was my Martin Sketchmore.

'Sassenach who thinks he's Scottish. Balding, likes his rugby and his pros?'

It was as good a description as I had heard. What intrigued me, on further interrogation, was that the meeting had occurred at a football event that was only a few years in the past. That put

Martin on this planet well after I thought Dupree had got to him.

I pumped Gerald for everything he knew but it wasn't much. He had met Martin at a Celtic supporters' do that was being held in Murrayfield – the home of Scottish rugby. They had got to talking at the bar. The inevitable subject of 1971 came up and then Martin had told Gerald that he always wanted to go to an Old Firm game but had never gotten round to it. Gerald happened to have two tickets for the main stand at Hampden for the upcoming Rangers v Celtic game in the Scottish Cup. The game was a sell out and tickets were nowhere to be found – not for love nor money. A few drinks later and they were soul mates. A few more and Gerald invited Martin to the game.

Gerald and Martin had drunk themselves stupid at the game but parted ways with no exchange of details. Martin had been a stranger to Gerald ever since. But it was enough for me. If Martin was alive someone would know where and I intended to find out.

It took me months of favours and back-handers to track him down. In truth it wasn't difficult, just agony when you are trying to do it from prison. My lack of friends made everything expensive, painful or slow.

I found out he was back in Glasgow and now part of the law abiding citizenry. He had a job in a city lawyers, as a 'by the hour' detective. His job was to dig up dirt and his old contacts had made him a bit of a winner at the gig. I knew he lived in Eaglesham - a small satellite village south of

Glasgow. I didn't have an address but with a name like Sketchmore I reckoned he wouldn't be too hard to find.

I took the bus to the village. A long haul by any accounts, and, when I arrived, I realised this might be harder than I first thought. The village, although small, was still big enough to cause me some grief and as I alighted the bus and stood next to the bus stop I thought - where now?

The pub was the obvious start point and I entered the Eaglesham Arms with some hope in my chest. Ten minutes later I was back on the street.

The bar staff had looked at me with the sort of blank expression reserved for non locals and people who weren't buying. The two customers I quizzed gave me even less than that. If I'd had a mobile in my pocket I could have given directory enquiries a pop but I could hardly afford the bus fare, never mind a mobile phone.

I wandered back up the main drag and headed towards the shops the bus had passed as it had entered the village. On my left I found a Chinese restaurant and a light bulb went on. Martin was big on his Chinese food. His tastes might have changed but I didn't think so.

The restaurant was small but welcoming. It was too early in the day for a crowd but there were still a few tables buzzing with chat. A matronly looking Chinese woman appeared to take my order and I had to disappoint her. I explained that I was a friend of Martin's just back from the big smoke and that I'd had my bag stolen on the train north. I knew he lived in Eaglesham but I didn't have his address – could they help?

She drew me a blank and I thought I was out on my backside but one of the diners had ear wigged the conversation, and beckoned me over. The Chinese lady threw him a look of disdain but he either missed it or didn't give a rats. He told me that Martin didn't live in Eaglesham but in a smaller village up the road called Jackton. He didn't know the address but he described the house and with thanks I was gone.

Jackton turned out to be a fair walk but its size made finding Martin's house easy and I stared at the front door for an age.

A decade earlier I would have envisaged myself kicking the door in and confronting him. I had envisaged myself beating him within an inch of his life. Dark night after dark night I dreamed of this moment - and then some - but now I just wondered what the hell I was doing here. Did I really need his help to crack the Credit Union? After all wasn't it just a toy town bank? The answer was no – it wasn't and I was scraping the bottom of a fairly deep barrel. One that had given up everything but Martin. After this I was a busted flush.

I stared at the door and thought - this is the bastard that had put me away for the best part of fifteen years. This is the man that had hung me out in a way that was hard to fathom.

I could still see him in the dock spouting forth – me open-mouthed as he spat out every tiny detail. He never looked at me once. Not even the swiftest of glances. He fixed his eyes on a spot behind the prosecuting lawyer and kept them there.

Not that he couldn't feel my gaze. It was a laser burning into his head - a laser loaded with all the hate I could muster. Yet he was an unblocked dam of information that flooded across the courtroom and drowned me.

As I stood at the door and looked at my watch I thought about all the time that the bastard had taken away. Every single second that could never be handed back. How he had walked free from the court and I had walked away in handcuffs. Him to a future outside prison walls. Me to one inside. And what would this visit achieve? After all he had sent the letter. Whatever lay in the safety deposit box was surely known to him. Yet there lay the intrigue. If he did know, then why give it to me? Bad news seemed the most logical conclusion. I was to be set up again. Was that it? Am I supposed to open the box and the contents lead me straight back to prison - or worse? Why else would he lead me to the key?

I know the bastard well. Is this his back up plan? His security blanket. Send me right back in. Go straight to jail - do not pass go. But why? He must have known I would look for him now I was out.

Before the Castlemilk and Easterhouse jobs I'd considered tracking him down, but it chewed my gut like cancer to think about it. Now I had no choice. Whatever lay in that box was going to be revealed. Either right now, right here or, with Martin's help, after I did Drumchapel.

I kicked the door. One way or another the mystery ended here. At least that's what I thought at that moment. As it turned out life is far from that simple.

The door flew open and Martin stood before me. Less hair, stooped and a good four stone heavier but it was Martin. If I expected shock at my presence it wasn't to be. He smiled as recognition took hold and, standing back, asked if I still took two sugar and milk. It was far from the response I had been expecting.

I walked into the house and was swallowed by an idyllic cottage - layout replete with large open hearth fire, overstuffed armchair and bright chintzy curtains over lattice windows. The floor was stone with a large rug dead centre and a couple of two seat sofas sat at right angles to each other. The ceiling was low and stripped with beams that made ducking a necessity for anyone over two feet tall. The walls were rough hewn sandstone and, opposite the fire, was a monumental sideboard and display cabinet. Just at that moment a grandfather clock chimed.

All of this would have been perfectly normal if it wasn't for the fact that I was standing in one of a small row of ex-council nineteen sixties, breezeblock homes. It was hard to fathom the dichotomy of exterior and interior but Martin resolved it in seconds.

'I bought it like this. The previous owners were in their eighties. They always wanted a farmhouse but couldn't afford it. So they did this. You should see the bedrooms. Drink?'

I almost missed the offer but the sound of glass on glass as Martin whipped two tumblers from the drinks cabinet meant we had moved on from tea to something stronger. I nodded my head. Martin waved at one of the sofas and I sat down. He chinked and clinked until a four-finger measure of whisky and ice appeared over my shoulder.

'Highland Park. Or have you changed.'

I hadn't had a glass of Highland Park malt whisky since the day before I was arrested. I gave a non-committal grunt and took a slug. Nectar slid down my throat and I realised how far I had fallen.

Martin sat down in the other sofa and sipped at a whisky that was half the size of mine. He kicked out his feet and let rip with a sigh that would have brought a tear to a glass eye.

'I'm surprised you didn't start off by kicking my head in,' he said.

'So am I.'

'A lot of questions?'

'Sorry.'

'You'll have a lot of questions?'

'No shit.'

'Fire on.'

This was not going in any shape or form the way I had planned it. For a start Martin was supposed to be quaking in his boots at my reappearance. At the moment the only quaking going on was the rumble of the double decker buses and trucks that occasionally went past his front door. I took another swallow and realised I had drained the glass. Martin pulled in his feet, stood up and took the glass from me. Clink, chink and it was full again.

'You must have been thirsty?'

I ignored the jibe.

I wasn't sure where to start. Did I get into the whole trial and betrayal thing? Did I ask how he had survived the coming to power of Dupree? Would an opening gambit be to ask about the key? Did I ask him if Partick Thistle were doing well or did I ask after his other love - rugby?

'How's Clarkston RFC doing?' I said.

'They aren't. They vanished years ago. Merged and changed names a few times and are now known as GHA. Still in the same place but a health club bought some land off them and, as part of the deal, they had a new stand and clubhouse built for them. Good deal really.'

'Do you still go to see them?'

'Most weekends when they are at home. Occasionally on the road but only if they are close by.'

'Any of the old school still there.'

'A couple. Jimmy Naismith still pulls the odd stint on coaching but he has a place in Spain and is more there than here. Donald Grier is club secretary but I am a bit persona non gratis with him. What with me and his daughter.'

I couldn't help laughing. Mary Grier had been an on/off girlfriend of Martin's for the last few years before I was sent down. Although she lived in Glasgow, Martin would fly her down for long weekends and then some. This seriously pissed of her dad – a lay preacher of the fire and brimstone variety. Donald was none to happy at his 'takeaway' daughter. His phrase not mine – 'You're like a bloody Indian takeaway. He calls and you deliver.'

Inevitably it had ended in tears when Martin, tired of the old man's complaints, found that Donald was badmouthing him to anyone that would listen. Donald had even been known to bring Martin's name into some of his sermons. Martin reacted by sending four of the lads to have a quiet word. Donald got the message but some people just don't scare well and he continued to slag off Martin. Only the intervention of his daughter saved him a more serious kicking.

'Do you still see Mary?'

'Kind of.'

'Meaning.'

'I see her when I pick up Tara.'

'Who's Tara?'

'Mary's stepdaughter.'

'Why would you be bothered about Mary's stepdaughter?'

'We're an item.'

'You and Mary's stepdaughter. No shit?'

I didn't ask her age. I could guess. Martin was just too weird for cheese.

The conversation drifted and was taking on a strange glow. Not just as a result of the whisky but, although we'd had our ups and downs, because we had always been able to gab just fine. The years were slipping away and my desire to lay into him was waning with the bottle.

'Hungry?'

I realised I was ravenous.

'Kind of.'

Martin reached for a cordless phone that sat next to his sofa and dialled a number from memory.

'For delivery please. Martin Sketchmore. Hi Ajmal. How's business? Good - can I have a Lamb Korma, Chicken Tikka Masala and two fried rice? Add in a garlic nan, a regular nan and a bottle of Diet Coke'

He hung up.

'Not Chinese?' I said.

'Had one last night.'

We jawed about next to nothing for half an hour before the doorbell went and we were in Indian food land. We ate in silence and when the dishes were cleared away and my glass refilled we sat down to some serious talk.

'The courtroom. Why?' I asked.

Martin rubbed his stomach and belched.

'Dupree had me by the nuts. I grass on you or my family/friends/acquaintances/colleagues/people I met when I was three and have never seen since - don't see the next morning. He threatened to kill mum, gran, Joan, Colleen - even little Brian. All of them and then some. What would you have done?'

I had always suspected as much but it didn't lessen my anger.

'You could have run.'

'Where? Dupree is an evil fucker. Far worse than you or me ever were. He was onto me hours after you were lifted and laid it on the line. You or my family.'

'So who cut the deal with the police?'

'Dupree. Don't ask me how, but he did.'

'And you believed he would keep his word?'

'It was my biggest fear. I drop you in it and then I'm history. But he's a weird one. His word is his bond. He said that not me. From what I know he seems to hold to that. If I stay away from him he'll honour our deal. How else could I have survived? I'm hardly the invisible man. How long did it take you to find me?'

That was true. I had found out his location from behind the bars of a prison. Dupree would have found him in seconds.

'The letter?' I said.

'Do you still have it?'

I pulled it out of my pocket and handed it to him. He rolled it up and threw it in the fire.

'So what's in the box?' I asked.

'I don't know. But whatever it is it didn't come from me '

'Sorry.'

'It's from Spencer. Whatever is in the box is from Spencer.'

'Where's Spencer?'

'Dead.'

'Dupree?'

'No, a car crash on the road to Oban about two years after you went down. Up until that point Spencer worked for Dupree.'

'I thought he vanished with you.'

'That's what Dupree wanted everyone to think but Dupree needed someone who knew the way the crockery was laid out until he could get his feet under the table. So Spencer was shipped back north and moved in with his mum in Inveraray. Dupree used him as a sounding board and as long as he kept himself to himself Dupree left him alone.'

I had known Spencer's mum had roots in Scotland but not where she lived. Inveraray was a tourist stop on the way to the Mull of Kintyre. Nice enough for the day but not somewhere I would choose for home and certainly not somewhere for Spencer. He would have gone out of his mind with boredom. I could see him now – blind drunk at the wheel of some hot rod, hammering up the road between Inveraray and Oban. On a good day you need to take care on the road as it either twists and turns through the glens or hugs the shore. Forty feet artics are frequent and, at points, the road hardly accommodates a mini. Car crashes were all too common.

'So what has Spencer got to do with the box?'

'I was staying with one of Spencer's friends. She lived in Fulham. Spencer turns up at the door one day. He looks nervous and knows he is well outside the safe zone that Dupree has given him. He comes in but he doesn't sit down. He shouldn't be in London and he knows it. His eyes are all over the place. Like he is expecting someone to jump him any minute. He tells me that Stevie at the Lame Duck has something for me. I look at him as if he just landed from Mars. I ask him what he is on about. He says he knows some things about Dupree and has given Stevie instructions to hand it over to you or me. Then he leaves. Next thing I know he is on the inside page of the Daily Record as one of four that died in a high speed crash on the road to Oban.'

'So you went to Stevie?'

'No.'

'Why?'

'You don't know Dupree. You really don't. He has figured out ways to hurt people that wouldn't seem credible in a Stephen King novel. I was safe and I wanted to stay that way but I figured you might like a pop at him. So I scribbled up the letter and sent it to you.'

'And you never once thought to see Stevie in all those years?'

'Oh it passed my mind now and again and I always reckoned that if I got a sniff Dupree was on the turn I could track down Stevie double quick.'

Sometimes in life you smell things that just makes your nose curl up.

'Are you telling me that you never went to find out what Stevie had been given?'

'Never. I wrote you the letter years ago and sent Rachel to deliver it when I thought you were due out. Then I tried to blank it from my mind.'

I rolled back in the chair and sipped at the malt. Martin was looking at me, waiting for a response but I didn't have one. Not then anyway. I sipped some more and held up the glass for more. Tonight was going no further. I either got very drunk or I went home.

I got very drunk.

Wednesday January 30^h 2008

I haven't felt like using the digital recorder for a few days. I know I promised myself to detail everything I did but I can't decide if the Drumchapel job is a worthwhile exercise.

I spent the night at Martin's and woke up the next morning less sure of my actions than I had been since I left prison. The last week has been a haze. My cell mates go on the batter nightly and I have avoided it like the plague. It would be too easy to slide into the alcohol wagon and tell everyone else to take a flying fuck.

On the night after my visit with Martin I was in a different place. I sat next to the Necropolis and stared down at Glasgow. Did I need this shit anymore? Would life be easier if I just dropped to first gear and wandered through the rest of my natural existence with little more horizon than the next bottle of booze? How hard could it be? How bad could it be?

I sat with my back against the grave of Hugh Tennent and looked at his brewery sprawled out at my feet and made a call. An hour later I was trying straight meths for the first time in my life. One taste and I threw up. I told the assembled body to sit tight and took off in the direction of Alexandra Parade. On the way I picked up a chunk of metal from a building site and entered the corner store with a face that said don't fuck with me.

I left with six bottles of malt – the store's entire inventory of good whisky. I made it clear to the shopkeeper that calling the police was not an option.

I put on the look of a man that had been here a million times before and the owner let me go quietly. When I returned to my drinking mates they were gobsmacked but they asked few questions as they tucked into the booty.

I fell asleep next to Hugh's grave. I think he might have understood.

For the next five nights I played the Tesco delivery van to my drinking companions' needs. I did in five stores and left each one in no doubt to the future should they call foul. Last night I drew a line in the sand and stepped back.

It wasn't hard to see why. My mates – now up to fifteen in number - were waiting on me behind the car impound on High St. Six of them were from the hostel but the others had joined our merry throng as my supply of drink had grown in notoriety. In the circles I was now mixing in, notoriety spreads fast.

I had eight bottles of varying sprits on me but after an hour it wasn't enough. My friends looked to me for more and, even in my inebriated state, I knew this was no way to a good place.

I pissed off and went up to the Necropolis to throw up. As I lay looking at the red tinged clouds above the city I knew I was on a bad slope and either I changed or I'd end up at the back end of a bottle for the rest of my life. The next day I went back to Martin's. This time I wanted his help and he had no choice over whether he gave it to me or not.

He opened the door and looked at me the way my mum used to look at me when I had been in a fight. The Highland Park was still on tap and I should have said no but I didn't. I needed something to kill the hangover.

We chatted and chewed the cud well into the night and the second bottle of malt was cracked open before I told Martin what I wanted. He looked at me and stood up. I was waiting for an exit stage left or a 'yes we are in this together'. Instead I got a blank and he headed for the toilet. I felt like a patient in a doctor's surgery waiting for results of a test. Martin came back in and looked at me.

'What's in it for me?'

Less than six months earlier I would have told him that keeping his life was a fair bargaining chip but the world moves on and I was in need of his help. What was in it for him? Why should he help me? After all if Dupree was such a bastard then a peaceful life in a mock farmhouse was no bad thing.

I was hardly in a position to offer a deal. What could I say? I'll breathe on you if you don't help? To be fair that was no idle threat given the state of my dental hygiene at the moment. I could stun at ten feet. Then I dug deep and went for the nuts.

'We shake and go home?'

It was a low blow. Not that low blows meant much now. It was a phrase I had used more than once in London.

When I had asked him to come down at first it was more than a request and he knew it. He had a good life in Glasgow and I was asking him to chuck it on the fire and head for my voice. To his credit he had done so, but not without a hundred regrets. I had shat on him from a high place and even though he had done well in London he was never happy.

Every time we had to put on the fight mitts I would tell him that it would soon be over and we could shake and go home. We never did. And now I was calling in a favour that didn't exist and he knew it. I stared at the whisky and was lost for words. My fall from grace was complete.

Martin walked behind me and reached down, grabbing my shoulders.

He could have taken me by the throat and who would have cared. Me? Not then. Not right at that moment. I waited on his fingers around my throat but of course they never came.

'You can't offer me home. I'm home but if I help you, we call it all quits.'

I looked up at him. The thinnest of smiles on my face.

'Deal.'

We turned to the options for Drumchapel in the same way we had planned a thousand jobs. As usual the first ideas were of the bog standard type - they always are.

I went on a creativity training course once – it was the old man's idea down in London. He had been on it and thought his direct reports should go. I thought he was kidding but it was a three-line whip and, as it turned out, a real eye opener.

I'm a cynical bastard about such things but it was better than I feared and a few things stuck in my head. One of them was what they call the 'First Burst' - the first ideas you come up with. The same old same old.

The course had told me that this was the norm and to get fresh thinking you needed to push by these ideas and, as none of the stuff we came up with answered the brief, we ploughed on. Then Martin threw in a wild idea and we were home free with added sugar. It always works that way.

We are going for it tomorrow.

Friday February 1st 2008

So now I know what Spencer left for me. Getting it was a stroke of genius on Martin's part and so blindingly obvious that I am currently thinking about submitting myself for the thick as a plank award.

Martin phoned the Credit Union and asked what the procedure was for retrieving the contents of a box for someone who was deceased. The requirements were straight forward enough - a copy of the death certificate and proof that you were now the legal heir to the deceased's property.

The former was easy. A trip to the Martha St births, deaths and marriages office and we were away. Spencer Cline, deceased 14th March 1996, cause of death – automobile accident.

The next step was trickier. Martin phoned directory enquiries and asked for a Cline living in Inveraray. There was one match and he phoned the number. Mrs Cline answered the phone and things got awkward.

Martin had only met her once before at Glasgow Central Station when she had turned up with Spencer in tow after he had enjoyed a long weekend away from the troubles of London.

Martin explained who he was and apologised for not attending Spencer's funeral. He told her he had been out of the country for the last fifteen years and had just come back to find a letter from Spencer that had been held by a mutual friend. The letter said that Spencer had tried to return some old photographs that Martin had loaned him but, by then, he had gone abroad. For whatever reason Spencer had placed them in a safety deposit box under his own name and he needed her permission to open the box.

Mrs Cline wasn't stupid and the story sounded weak and probably sounded even weaker from her end of the phone. Martin tap danced for a few minutes and said he would be happy to send her the key and, next time she was in Glasgow, she could open the box and send the photos onto him. This tipped the balance. Mrs Cline was in her late eighties and a trip to Glasgow to open the box of her long dead son was not one she wanted to take.

She asked what she needed to do and Martin gave her the Credit Union number and told her he would phone back and asked her to release the box in his name. If they needed it in writing then could she send the letter to the Credit Union and he would go along sometime next week.

Martin phoned back an hour later and I heard him thank her for transferring the box.

Martin drove to the Credit Union and I rode side saddle. He was inside for less than ten minutes and returned to the car with an envelope. He handed it to me as he got in and I fingered it. He pulled out of the mall car park and slipped into the late afternoon traffic.

The envelope was standard size but it was bulked out and the mouth was sealed with tape that had yellowed with age. There was enough of a seal to let me know that no one had opened it in a long time.

I ran my finger along the opening and pulled away the tape, tipping the contents onto my lap and Martin glanced over. There was a single sheet of folded typed paper, an old four inch floppy disc and a smaller envelope. I opened the smaller envelope and a bunch of Polaroid photos tumbled out. I held one up and, although faded with age, the darkness of the envelope had saved them for disappearing altogether.

The photo showed four men sitting at a table, drinks in front of them. They could easily have been abroad as the table had the ubiquitous Coca Cola parasol above it and two of the men were wearing sunglasses.

I recognised Dupree but not the other three - although there was something familiar about two of them. I flicked through the other photos and they were all of the same scene save one that showed the four men leaving a building. Dupree was at the back and the other three were out front. Dupree was looking to the left and two of the other men were looking to the right. The last man was looking at something in the foreground.

All four were dressed like the hit squad from Reservoir Dogs. If they had wanted to draw attention to themselves they were making a good job of it. There was no date on the photos but with Spencer dead twelve years then they were at least from that far back.

I opened up the paper to find it contained nine numbers typed neatly in the centre followed by four stars.

13,5,79,111,315,1,71,921,2,****

The numbers meant nothing to me. I picked up the floppy disc but the label was blank.

'Well?' said Martin

'I have no idea. There are some pictures of Dupree with some friends. A floppy disc that probably pre dates Microsoft and a letter with some numbers on it.'

'Who are the friends?'

'I've no idea although there is something familiar about two of them but nothing I can put my finger on at the moment.'

'Maybe the disc has some more info.'

'Maybe.'

We drove back to Martin's in silence and I flicked through the photos but the two faces that seemed familiar kept on their mask of anonymity.

We arrived at the house as the sun gave in for another day and I lifted myself from his car with effort.

Once inside, Martin cracked another bottle of Highland Park and poured. I knew there were fewer bottles in the cupboard than he was letting on to but I still accepted the liquid with barely a nod.

We dropped the photos on the coffee table and Martin grabbed the typed sheet. I sipped on the malt and lifted up the photo of the four leaving the building.

I squinted in the artificial cottage light and reached behind me and pulled a Pixar angle poise lamp a little closer. I was no longer interested in the four men in the picture - the building behind was now the focus of my attention. I threw the photo to Marin.

'What does the plaque to the left of Dupree say?'

Martin looked at the photo and then pulled the lamp towards him.

'Not sure. Caixa maybe? What the hell does Caixa mean?'

'Ever been to Spain?'

'A couple of times. Lads' holidays mostly.'

I took another slug of the Highland cream.

'Well I owned a place out there and Caixa is well familiar.'

Martin looked at me.

'Bank, my dear friend. It means bank. Now look a little closer.'

Martin pulled the photo up until it sat a few inches from his nose.

'Col, col – can't read it but it looks like Col something – Col. Caixo.'

'Colonya Caixa,' I said. 'Our esteemed friend has some interest in the Spanish banking system.'

I drained the glass and let the fluid take its course. Smooth, balanced - with a rich full flavour and a gentle smokey finish - well that's what I was told once by a whisky nut - it warmed my stomach.

'I've no idea what the photo means but Spencer didn't leave this stuff for the hell of it. If I know anything of the devious prick, he has handed us Dupree on a plate. Trouble is I don't know what restaurant the plate belongs to.'

It was time for home. I asked Martin to call a taxi and then to add insult to injury asked him for the fare.

Hey life's a bitch.

Monday February 4th 2008

Martin came round today. I'd had a bad weekend and, to be fair, he wasn't an unpleasant sight. I had spent most of Saturday and all of Sunday going back over the photos and the letters.

I asked the computer geek if he had access to an old floppy drive and he told me that a friend still had a steam powered computer and laughed. I kicked him in the ankle and he went off to sulk.

I tried the libraries but floppy discs are long since gone and on Sunday night I was back talking to the geek about his friend. He said if I gave him the disc he would print off what was on it. I told him to take a running jump. After a bit of negotiation we are going to see the geek's friend tonight.

The photos must have some significance but not knowing the faces other than Dupree makes them frustrating. I'm sure I've seen two of the others before but it won't come back. The fact that the photos are probably taken in Spain doesn't help or hinder.

I had a place in Spain. Note the word *had*. It lay just south of Malaga on the Costa Del Sol. When I bought the thing it was one of four in a block built by a local builder. Swimming pool to the front and a good quarter of a mile of scrubland between the houses and the beach.

I have no idea what the area looks like now but even on my last visit, and that goes back fifteen odd years, the place had changed beyond recognition.

The scrubland was gone - replaced with acre after acre of villas and apartments. To the rear a new development stretched to the main road a mile back and the front, which had been a wild beach when I first moved in, was now a parade with the usual array of restaurants, shops and other nonsense.

The bank in the photo rings no bells. I used a UK bank with a branch in Malaga when I was in Spain.

Martin sat on the front step of the hostel with me and pulled out a quarter bottle of Bells. I pushed it back into his pocket, stood up and told him to follow me. We walked round the hostel and up towards the Necropolis and I pointed to a bench that was overhung by an old oak tree.

'House rules,' I said. 'No drink in or near the hostel. If you are caught you get a warning. Next time you're out.'

Martin laughed.

'You are kidding. Most of the guys in there must be a bottle down by lunch time. Do they not see the irony?'

'Of course but rules are rules and if you want a bed you stick by them. Also booze in the hostel is a shit idea. Fights break out. You'd be amazed what some of the guys will do to get their hands on a bottle of juice.'

Martin shrugged and passed the bottle over to me. It wasn't malt but it would do.

'Any joy with the photos or the disc?'

I told him about the planned visit to the geek's friend and he asked if he could tag along. I couldn't see why not.

'I've a thought on the photos,' he said. 'When you went down I spent a few weeks in London before bailing out. Dupree ignored me. We had a deal and as far as he was concerned I either stuck to it or I was dead. However, on a couple of occasions, one of Dupree's lads paid me a visit. Usually to pick my brains over some bit of business or other. One of the visitors was a young Spanish lad. I can't remember his name but he was an eager beaver. Let me see the photos?'

I pulled them out and he stared at them.

'Look. The photo at the bank. There's Dupree at the back and you reckon you might know who the guy to the left and the guy to the right are? It's hard to tell but the guy in the front looks Spanish to me.'

'Your lad?'

'Could be. He's younger than the other three by a fair number of years and the sunglasses don't help.'

'And?'

'Well the eager beaver let drop that his dad was something big in Spain. An ex pat who had fled in the seventies. He married a local and then came the eager beaver.'

'Who's the ex pat?'

'He never said but I tell you who went out in the seventies and married a local - Tommy Ryder.'

I stopped mid-swallow and coughed the liquid back up.

'Ryder. Ryder's involved with Dupree?'

'I said I'm not sure. I never really bothered back then. I had a lot on my mind but there was something familiar about the young Spanish lad, I just never put two and two together until the photos appeared.'

'Ryder,' I said. 'That would make a fuck load of sense.'

Tommy Ryder had been one of the No Mean City crew in Glasgow during the sixties. A bastard and, as I found out, the guy behind 'the Nose's' early demise.

He had played hard and won hard right into the seventies and then, when everything got that much more complicated, he jumped ship to Spain. Over the years his name came up, usually when something shit went down on my patch. He might have moved to Spain but he was still a mover in Glasgow.

I met him once. It was at the funeral of an old ex con called Si Parker. A con artist of the old school - a brilliant impersonator and right up to his dying days was still a great bet for many a role. If Si hadn't been a con he would have been an actor.

It was risky for Ryder to come home but Si was up there as one of the guys that had taught a young Ryder all he knew. He flew in by private plane, went to the funeral and flew out. I wouldn't even have known he was there if he hadn't sidled up to me outside the church and shook my hand.

'I hear you're doing well? Nice to see some new talent on the block.'

The man doing the talking looked more like a tramp than a rich ex pat. He smelled bad as well. Thick beard, droopy eyes and a coat too warm for the time of year. Si would have been proud of the disguise. There were close on ten police in the crowd trying to spot Si's old associates and Ryder walked out right under their noses.

'So, if Ryder is tied up with Dupree what the hell is the point of the photos? It's hardly going to make headline news that someone like Dupree has a tie up with a bastard like Ryder,' I said.

'True. So I'll be guessing the bit that Spencer was interested in doesn't lie with our Spanish boy. You said you thought you knew who the other two were so it's over to you.'

I sipped at the bottle and stared at the photos but there was no magic light bulb. I flicked from photo to photo and then halted.

'Ryder didn't do the Malaga run, did he?'

In the seventies a lot of Brits ran for Spain - under Franco there was no extradition from Spain and a community had sprung up on the Costa Del Sol of some of the UK's most wanted.

Martin looked at me and grabbed the bottle for a swig.

'Not Malaga - Majorca I heard.'

'Off the beaten track as well,' he added. 'Not by the sea. I remember thinking it was an odd thing to do. Back then you could have had your pick of beauty spots for next to fuck all so why pick a place in the middle of nowhere?'

'Maybe his Spanish lady wanted to be close to mum.'

'I think I even know the town?'

'What after thirty years?'

'Yeah. After the funeral Si's brother came up to say thanks for coming. He said that Ryder had offered him a job in Spain if he wanted to quit the rain and early closing hours. I asked if he was taking it and he said maybe. He reckoned it was Ryder's way of saying thanks to Si.'

'So where did he go?'

'I know this sounds stupid but I'm sure he was off to Inca.'

'What as in Peru, Machu Pichu and pan pipes?'

'Same name but it was a village in the middle of Majorca - always stayed with me that name - don't know why. I always thought I'd look it up if I was in Majorca but I never was.'

'So the photos were taken in Majorca?'

'Mallorca if you want to be more accurate. Could be. Maybe even in Inca?'

'What the hell would Dupree want with some out of the way town on Mallorca?'

'No idea but it's a start. I reckon the disc will tell us more.'

I took the bottle back from him and drained it.

Tuesday February 5th 2008

The geek's friend is even more of a geek than the geek. I've seen less high tech computer gear on the bridge of the USS Enterprise. He lives in a flat in Shawlands on the south side of Glasgow.

Shawlands is where the south side of Glasgow tries to be the west end and fails. For my money I prefer the south - less pretentious. Being pretentious in Glasgow marks you out as an industrial strength prick and there are few more pretentious than some that live in the west end - of course there are a few exceptions to the rule and you don't have to go far south in Glasgow to find the seriously deluded.

Let's just say that Glasgow has a golden S that runs through it. From the north west to the south east. All the best areas can claim some place within the S. If you take the start and the finish of the S - you'll not be far from the 'fur coat and nae knickers' brigade. I know I used to be a resident.

The geek's flat was wall to wall with wires, boxes (plastic and pizza) and screens. He took the disc from me like it was a child's nappy and sighed. The sigh seemed to indicate that such technology was beneath him but I assumed he had been informed by the geek of the pain that refusing to help might incur.

He wandered over to a corner of the room and after a suitably long period of groaning and moaning dragged out a disc drive and a computer with the words Tiny embossed in the side.

'Nae point firing this sod up on a new machine. This is pre W 95. If my old Tiny still works she'll read it fine.'

He plugged the box into the mains and spent ten minutes doing a wire thing. The machine took another ten minutes to crank itself into life. We weren't offered coffee but given the geek's friend was even less conscious of his personal hygiene than the geek I thought this a good thing.

At last the screen settled down and the geek's friend pushed the disc into the drive.

'The Tiny's drive is screwed. I hope the bolt on works.'

It did and the first thing it came up with was a flashing icon and four stars.

'It needs a password.'

I looked at him and he looked at me.

'How hard can it be?' I said.

'Depends. If it is some crappy kid's toy - no problem. But even in the nineties (he said nineties the way I would talk about my grandpa in the war) they could write a half decent protection protocol. We enter the wrong password and I'm in for a night or two of fun. It might just lock me out altogether.'

I pulled out the folded piece of paper and showed him the numbers. His eyes lit up. Four stars on the paper and four stars on the screen.

13,5,79,111,315,1,71,921,2,****

'Sad, man. Really sad.'

The geek's friend typed in four numbers and the disc whirred and brought up a menu. I couldn't help myself.

'How did you figure the code so quick?'

The geek's friend smiled. He took the numbers and said 'Move the commas.'

He did so and 13,5,79,111,315,1,71,921,2,**** became 1,3,5,7,9,11,13,15,17,19,21,2****.

'What do you think comes next?'

I could have kicked him but I'd wait until he got to the bottom of the disc's innards before I took out his legs.

The contents of the disc turned out to be less revealing than I had hoped. There were two files on it, both of the Word variety. The geek's friend's computer ground away. Each document had one page and each page had a few characters typed in the middle. The printer whirred and it spat out both sheets.

Sheet one read:

ATV9AXLPCIU4D8I3AT9RIPNLC4A903753
Q0201

Sheet two was no less cryptic

C2O5M3PIT9EF1G3H211L4LAXLFATCOOO
NTTARCAPS9E4NDYYARR1Y4DFETR

I stared at both sheets.

'What the fuck is that?'

I always did have a nice turn of phrase.

They both shrugged and I folded the papers and put them in my pocket. The geek's friend passed me the disc and we were out of there.

I headed for Martin and his dwindling supply of Highland Park.

Wednesday February 13th 2008

I'm losing interest in the whole thing. Digital recordings, mystery letter from Spencer - even Martin's lure has dwindled since he ran out of malt. I've spread the photos and the sheets of paper in front of me so often my neighbours think they are porn. I can't make head nor tail of it and I'm beginning to wonder if it is worth the candle.

After all, crossing swords with Dupree earned me nothing but a locked door and bars on the windows for fourteen years. Even if I can figure out what Spencer had discovered, who is to say Dupree won't just finish the job and have me done in. It's certainly the advice that Martin has being doling out and it seems a far easier option than taking this nonsense any further. At least it did until last night.

I was sitting on the steps of the hostel when the manager wandered out.

'Need to get you moving.'

I didn't realise he was addressing me and I continued to stare at the pavement.

'They are closing this place down for a refurb in two weeks. It will be shut for three months. I'm struggling to place you all. Have you anyone that you can move in with?'

I looked up, realising that I was the intended recipient of the words. I shook my head.

'You'll have to find somewhere. Even when we reopen you won't get back in. We are changing this place to emergency accommodation only. If you want to stay you are going to need to re-apply each night. So if I were you I would start thinking about a place to live and maybe a job?'

The last word came out with a laugh attached to it. I smiled back but I really wanted to cave his head in.

So I am out on the street - literally. I have no cash, no roof and sod all prospects. It was just then that I thought 'fuck it - I may as well go after Dupree' - what the hell else is left?'

I blagged some bus fare off the geek and headed for Martin's.

To my surprise he was in. I had expected to camp out in his garden, waiting for him to come home, but he had cut work early as he was going to a concert that night. He was off to see Babyshambles at the Barrowlands.

'Bit old for Pete Docherty aren't you?'

'When did you get your pension?'

'Piss off.'

I asked if I could use his house for the evening. One way or another I needed to figure out my next move. Martin had access to the internet - which was fine except I had no idea how to use the thing. Inside prison I had shunned it and since I got out I had avoided it. I asked Martin for a crash course. He introduced me to the wonders of Google and told me he would be back by twelve o'clock.

'And leave the fucking whisky alone.'

I told him I would and he knew I wouldn't.

I made a cup of tea and spread the photos and sheets on the table.

The four photos I placed on the left, the two sheets of printed paper in the centre and the tea on the right. I took a scribble pad from Martin's cupboard and bunch of pens.

I went back to the photos first. Martin had a magnifying glass in the cupboard and with a nod to Sherlock Holmes I picked up each photo and scanned them one by one.

The three at the café were duds. There was barely enough detail to make out the faces never mind a clue to where they were. The one outside the bank gave up little but the internet provided me with a hit.

The only bank I could find that matched the plaque was Colonya Caixa de Pollenca. Their web site was in Spanish or Catalan but not English. I was sure that with the wonders of the internet that this could be translated, but I was still crawling in my Pampers when it came to using the web.

The site indicated they had a number of branches in Mallorca but as to which one Dupree was standing outside was no clearer.

I picked up the magnifying glass and poured over the photo again. Then my head went pop.

'Inca, fucking Inca.'

I went back to the web site and looked at the bank's details and sure enough there was a branch in Inca. Colonya Caixa de Pollenca, Av Alcudia 9, Inca, 07300. I punched the air.

So they were in Inca - Ryder's home town - it made sense. I put the photos to one side and picked up the two sheets of paper.

ATV9AXLPCIU4D8I3AT5RIPNLC4A903753 Q0201

C2O5M3PIT9EF1G3H211L4LAXLFATCOOO
NTTARCAPS9E4NDYYARR1Y4DFETR

Gibberish. If they were a code then there had to be a key.

I took the shorter string of characters and played around with the letters and the numbers for an hour. Taking a breather I raided Martin's drinks cabinet before I went back to it again, but got nowhere.

I remembered the creativity course I had been on and it advised leaving the problem alone, doing something else and then going back to it with a fresh head. I fired up the TV and used a film on TCM to drain my brain.

I must have fallen asleep. When I woke up the film was near the end. It was a poor man's Jimmy Cagney and I wasn't interested but just as I went to kill the telly, the central character pulled open a door and leapt in, gun at the ready.

The baddie (or it could have been the goodie) was waiting.

'Can't pull the same stunt twice Mikey.'

With that he shot the goodie (or baddie) in the chest. Shit dialogue - I turned it off but the same stunt twice line ran through my head and then an Edison sized light bulb went on. I pulled out the sheet of paper with the disc code on it and grabbed the sheet with

ATV9AXLPCIU4D8I3AT5RIPNLC4A903753
Q0201 on it.

1,3,5,7 and so on - what if the disc's owner had used this for the key as well as the code for the disc.

I scribbled down only the characters that related to the odd numbers.

It read

Avalcudia5inca07300 - or Av Alcudia 5, Inca, 07300

I cracked a bottle of seriously expensive wine ten seconds later. The next part was easy. I applied the same logic to the other sheet and came up with

compte13214alacontrasenyaryder.

It still looked like rubbish.

I slugged at the wine and sat back. Maybe the second sheet worked to a different code. I picked up the pen and tried another variant highlighting every even number - still gibberish. I tried every third number, every fourth. I tried starting with the second letter and choosing every third and fourth. I tried every fifth and then I tried the first number, the second number the fourth the eighth and so on.

Sheet after scribbled sheet ended up in a pile on the table. I threw none away. I wanted to ball each failure up and sling it in the bin but how was I to know that there weren't two steps to this and that the secret lay in taking an earlier attempt and applying another code.

I finished the bottle of wine and rested my head in my hands.

'My good wine, you bastard.'

I woke up to Martin shaking me. I looked at the clock. It was gone two o'clock.

'Sorry but I thought I had cracked this bloody code.'

I showed him the first sheet. He smiled or rather his lips moved up at the edges - it could have been a sneer but I was in alcohol fuzz mode.

He picked up the second sheet and I handed him my first attempt at decoding it. He looked at for a few seconds and then bent down. He placed the decoded sheet on the table, and spread it out trying to even out the creases and folds. He picked up a pen and circled the last five letters on it.

Ryder

We were left with.

compte13214alacontrasenya

'And?' I said.

'Give me a minute.'

He took the sheet over to the computer and typed the whole line into Google. I followed him over and watched as the screen came up with:

Your search - compte13214alacontrasenya - did not match any documents.

He laid the sheet next to the computer and doodled for a second before putting a ring around the letters 'compte', another ring round '13214' and a final ring around 'alacontrasenya'

He pumped 'compte' into Google. It produced a few hits - mostly to do with French. Martin brought up a French/English on line dictionary. He inputted the word and the translator spat out 'count' or 'amount'.

'French?' I said.

He ignored me. He entered the word Catalan and English in the Google box and got a site that translated 'compte' as 'account'. He put in 'alacontrasenya' into the site. It came up blank. He started to chew the pen and then entered 'a la contrasenya'. It blanked. He entered just 'contrasenya' and the site threw up 'password'.

He grabbed a new sheet and wrote:

Account - 13214 (a) (ala)

Password - ryder.

'Ta da. I think this is the account number and the password for the bank you found. I can't be sure of the account number because the 'a' and the 'la' may be part of the word 'contrasenya' or they may not.'

'How the hell did you get to Catalan?'

'Mallorca is connected in some way to Catalan - or something - I'm no expert. The first word was in French but Catalan and French have links and given the bank was in Mallorca I gave it a go. Amazing what you can do on the internet.'

'Clever,' I said, 'But the address for the Colonya Caixa de Pollenca in Inca is at number 9, not number 5 Alcudia Ave?

So there we finished and I wasn't sure how much closer to revenge on Dupree I was. We had a photo of four men - two of whom we knew. A connection to an old Glasgow criminal. An account number and password for a bank in Spain (maybe). And what?

It was too late for the hostel so I blagged the couch in Martin's room and fell asleep in seconds.

Friday February 15th 2008

It's strange how some things work out. I spent yesterday running over the evening at Martin's. The highs and lows of working through the puzzle. The resolution that turns out not to be a resolution but yet another puzzle.

I jumped a bus into the city centre and went for a walk, mindful that whoever was after me might know where I now lived and could be following. I kept to the busy parts of town and looked over my shoulder so often I must have looked like some day release patient from the local nut-shop pretending to be a spy on a secret mission.

In between the looks over my shoulder I ran through my head what I knew and decided it was nowhere near enough to make a decision on what to do next.

If Dupree's demise lay buried in the photos or hidden in the bank account, then better people than myself and Martin were needed. Such people exist and I may have been locked up for fourteen years but my network of contacts has not faded to the point where it is useless. Some of them are dead and some have moved on but there are enough around that could help if I wanted to raise my head above the parapet and call on them.

But therein lies the problem. I haven't contacted anyone because I want to keep my profile low - very low.

As I walked by the HMV record shop on Argyle St I caught the sound of The Beloved as they threw out the invitation to Lose Yourself In Me. Strange to hear a nineties band blaring out - maybe it was greatest hits season - although post Christmas seemed an odd time if it was.

I like The Beloved - chilled music before the term chilled was hijacked by the dance brigade as post drug come down music. Jon Marsh's voice always sounded the way I thought people would who only ever breathed out and I mouthed the words - probably adding to the lunatic cover I was building - mouthing, shoulder looks and the dress sense of Wurzel Gummidge - I was your friendly neighborhood fruit bat.

I was a yard past the front door to the store when it hit me. Lose Yourself In Me. It was exactly what I was doing to myself. I'd swapped one prison for another. One with physical bars for one with mental bars. I was free to wander the streets but I had no money, little human contact and soon no roof over my head.

I could see myself down on the river front, lying under the bridge with the other down and outs. I could taste the meths, smell the shit, feel the concrete under my bum. Ice cold in winter - stinking hot in the summer. I could see the spot in Buchanan St where I would squat down and hold out cupped hands waiting for someone to drop ten pence or spit on me.

I stopped walking and listened to the music. What was I doing? I'd once had a hell of a life and the balls to hold onto it. I was a millionaire. Ok a bent millionaire but I had the cash, the status and, best of all, a future and now I was shuffling around

Glasgow in rags. Next I'd start thinking about how long before death makes this all go away.

I focused my thoughts on Dupree and what the bastard had done to me. What was the down side of going after him? What in the hell was he going to do to me that I wasn't already doing to myself? Kill me. So what! Do nothing and I'd be dead in a year.

I turned and walked into the store and the security guard approached me.

'Can I help sir?'

I felt my shoulders drop as I started to turn to leave and then I stopped. I turned back and looked him in the eye. I had a couple of inches in height on him but he had a couple of tons of muscle that I would never see.

I did a Michael J Fox and flipped back in time. I dug out a part of me that had been locked away for a long time. I pulled up, from the depths, the way I used to think when someone fronted me up and dropped all the feeling from my eyes. I tipped my head to one side and balled up a fist. I rocked forward on the soles of my feet and closed the distance between me and the security guard. My breath was probably killing him. I lifted my balled up hand and stretched out a finger - touching him lightly on the shoulder.

'Going to have a look for some CD's. Is that a fucking problem?'

I saw the fear sprint over his face. I knew the look of old. I lifted my finger higher and touched him on the nose.

'Is it?'

I dropped my hand and walked into the shop. I knew he wouldn't shout. It felt good. A long way from being back on track but it felt good.

Maybe I'm not dead.

At least not dead yet.

Saturday February 23rd 2008

I have moved out of the hostel and in with Martin. I gave him no choice but to be fair he didn't give me any grief. I'm sitting here in a fresh pair of jeans, a Teetonic t-shirt, a pair of Timberland boots and a clean set of teeth. My hair is crew cut and the beard is gone. I have three hundred pounds sterling on my hip and access to a car. All courtesy of Martin's generous nature and the fact that I said I'll pay him back in less than a month.

I've yet to pull myself back into my old world but I know I will. I just need to do it with speed and purpose that suit the moment.

I haven't seen the goon patrol for a while but I can't believe that they would give in that easy. They'll be back but I don't give a monkey's at the moment. I have a plan of action. Not the best plan on the planet but any plan is better than no plan. It is built around three questions:

1) Who are all the people in the photos?
2) What is behind the bank account details?
3) Can I sink Dupree?

It's that simple. In true tit over arse fashion I'm starting with question 2 and I'm paying a visit to Charlie Wiggs on Monday.

Charlie was my last proper accountant. The man who manfully arranged my annual finances to make the Inland Revenue smile. Charlie was never on the inside track of what I did but he wasn't stupid enough to believe that my only source of income came from my 'consultancy' work - but hey in the eighties consultancy was the buzzword and it covered a multitude of sins.

I took me a while to track him down. He had moved on and now worked for a crowd called Cheedle, Baker and Nudge located in a forty storey monstrosity called Tyler Tower on West George St. Charlie lives on the twentieth floor and when I finally appeared at the reception I was met by a man with a walking stick.

'Charlie Wiggs. As I live and breathe,' I said.

'Shite.'

It's nice to know you're loved. Charlie had been busy. It transpires that he had become a bit of a celeb after nearly dying in George Square during a sting to catch an old friend of mine. When I say friend I really mean arsehole.

I got the full SP on the events surrounding his rise to sainthood and was impressed to find that Charlie had, along with a couple of friends, brought down a whole gang of criminals. In the process both his legs had been stabbed and the walking stick was the last crutch on the way back to full fitness.

It sounded like a hell of a story but I wasn't in the mood for a Jackanory moment and had told him what I wanted. He questioned me and I had to tell him more than I wanted to, but I needed the info. He told me to leave the bank details and come back Monday. I told him what would happen if word got out about our meeting and he took it on board.

Roll on Monday.

Tuesday February 26th 2008

I didn't get back until late last night so, coffee in hand and staring at Martin's tiny back garden, I'm dictating in a pair of boxers and nothing else. Martin is away to work and like the dutiful partner I have a list of chores that are expected of me before he returns. The list is sitting next to me, staring up, willing me to do nothing.

Charlie turned out to be a small gold mine of information. I had expected a brief chat on the vagaries of the Spanish banking system and some insight into how I might access the account. Instead Charlie gave me War and Peace.

'Ok,' he started. 'Let's go with the simple stuff first.'

We were sitting in a Costa coffee near Charlie's office. A soup bowl of double shot latte sat in front of him and I nursed a water - Martin's supply of good drink had all been exhausted by me the night before.

'The bank you gave me the details on is a well established, well respected member of the financial community. The Colonya Caixa de Pollenca has been around in one form or another since 1880. It was a single office for sixty years and only opened its first branch outside Mallorca in 2000. Even now the majority of the branches are in Mallorca but they now service all the Balearic Islands and also have presence in Barcelona.'

I'd forgotten what a briefing from Charlie was like. Martin used to call him University Charlie.

'They seem to be a modern and dynamic bank. Small but efficient and well established in the area. I phoned a friend of mine who has a flat in Puerta De Pollenca and he uses them for his Spanish account.'

I hadn't wanted Charlie to start phoning his mates but then again I hadn't told him not to.

'He rates them. I asked about the account system and it's fairly well a standard affair. They offer a range of accounts and they are all well protected. As such the information you have is next to useless.'

That got my attention.

'Useless?' I said. 'We have an account number and a password.'

'Fine as far as it goes. But they don't refer to any traditional account. I asked my friend and the account number is wrong. On top of this the only area he has a password for is the internet account he holds with them. It's called Colonya Directa but it needs a user name and password. Without the user name we are stuffed.'

'Look, if it is the account of the person I think it is we can guess the user name. I know a computer geek that would love this stuff.'

'It's not for me to throw cold water on your plans but even if you do guess the user name and the password matches there will be at least one other level of security - usually something like your favourite book or film - and whoever owns the account will have answered five or six such questions. If you get past the user name and password it will randomly throw one of the questions at you. Get it wrong too often and it kicks you out.'

I must have looked blank at this point.

'Don't you have an internet account?'

'Charlie, I can hardly spell internet.'

'Well even if the password is valid and you guess the user name and answer to the security question you are still gubbed because you don't have a valid account number. It's too short and no system will let you in without a valid account number or a customer number and you have neither.'

Talk about a bucket of sick being tipped on your breakfast.

'So that's that?'

Charlie smiled.

'Not necessarily. I did a bit of thinking. You say the account and password relate to the bank because of the photos?'

I nodded my head.

'What if they don't? What if the number and password refer to something else altogether?'

'Go on.'

'Well you said the number of the building on the avenue was wrong'

'So.'

'My friend asked me how many numbers were in the account number and he laughed. He told me it doesn't sound like an account number - more like a security code.'

'What kind of security code?'

'He told me that a few years ago a Brit on the island got the idea to start up a little security business. Security guards, bouncers etc. Not unusual but this business is thriving. Four or five years ago the company branched out from its single office in the capital of the island - Palma and opened offices around the island. On top of local security services, the offices offer things like alarm fitting, security fixtures for the home and, wait for it, safety deposit boxes.'

'My friend has one,' he continued. 'He says the process is simple. You take ID along to the local office. You sign in and then enter an account number followed by a password to get access to your box. He tells me that they are extremely popular with the Brits. Especially those keen to keep stuff in a secure place away from the prying eyes of a partner. The Spanish banks offer something similar but some Brits obviously have stuff that they would rather didn't sit in a Spanish institution.'

'And you think this account number and password would open a box in one of these offices.'

'It would fit if someone had something they didn't want anyone to see.'

I finished my water and sat back.

'How many offices does this firm have?'

Charlie reached into his briefcase and took out a couple of sheets of paper.

'I printed this off the internet this morning.'

I took the sheets. They were from a web site called www.mallorca-security.com. I was still gaining my web feet but the page seemed self explanatory.

'There's not much to the site. Quite thin really,' said Charlie. 'I would hope their offices are a bit more substantial. The web site makes them look like a shoe string operation.'

I read through the two sheets and asked if there was anymore.

'No that's it.'

The firm claimed it had been established in 1998 and had six branches throughout Mallorca. It listed the services it offered and encouraged you to phone one of the branches for more details. There was little more.

'Who owns the firm?' I asked.

'It's not on the web site but my friend says it's some Brit called Ryder.'

Ker-ching. A step forward. Mr Ryder had branched out into security. Now there was a surprise. I wondered just what kind of 'protection' he offered to his clients. I thanked Charlie and threatened him with bodily violence if he breathed a word of this to anyone.

'One last question. How would you know which branch the numbers and the password belong to?'

'I don't know but I could ask my friend.'

'Can you also find out which branches have security deposit boxes?'

As I left him I looked at the address for the branch in Inca - Av Alcudia 5.

Bingo.

Thursday March 6th 2008

The best laid plans and all that. My post HMV revival and my reinvigorated mission to bring down Dupree hit a roadblock of immense proportions.

I had decided that I needed to go to Spain. Charlie had come back to me and said that only two of the branches of Mallorca Security carried safety deposit boxes and one of those was in Inca.

I priced up flights and accommodation along with a car and came up someway short of the required readies. I tried to tap up Martin but this proved tricky. I told him about the meet with Charlie and he was none to happy. No reason. He just went south on me and clammed up. Conversation became a tough gig and he wouldn't let me in on his reason for the cold shoulder. I didn't have time to fart around so I went my own way.

Back to the tools as they say. Time for a little breaking and entering.

My small tool kit for the hostel was lightweight and I needed some decent stuff so I rolled up to the Barras, a match to the markets of Marrakech only with more diversity. I hadn't expected to pick everything up in one go and, in that, I was wrong.

It was Sunday afternoon and the place was just calming down from heaving. I had spotted a few likely stores and stalls with the sort of products I needed and was just about to put my hand in my pocket when I stumbled over a hardware stall with an owner who couldn't have looked dodgier had he been wearing a trilby, a trench coat and spoken like George Cole.

As soon as I enquired after the price of a couple of items he nodded to a boy playing a Nintendo DS to take over and he beckoned me behind the stall. He reached into a box, rooted around and pulled out a leather wrap.

'You wouldn't be looking for one of these would you, sir?'

'Sir' sounded so dismissive I almost smacked him one. Instead I took the wrap and laid it on the ground. Checking that no one could see, I undid the cord holding the leather together and rolled out the dog's bollocks of a tool kit. It made the one that I had half-inched at the hostel look like a kid's toy. A bit old school but there was only one use for the combination of tools that nestled in the wrap and the owner knew it. I fingered the tools, each held in place by its own piece of hand sewn leather.

I rolled it back up and stood up.

'Bit old fashioned,' I said.

'Premium kit though sir.'

'Price?'

'One hundred'

I laughed.

'Twenty five.'

He laughed and I laughed and we both laughed all the way to sixty quid.

Next on the list was a target. In the old days this was easy. We had informers falling over themselves to tell tales of the riches locked away in homes. With no one to help, I went back to the shoe leather and picked an affluent end of town and spent a couple of days walking the streets and a couple of nights walking the back gardens.

I had narrowed my thoughts down to one of three houses and was sitting in the back garden of my first choice, trying to figure out the security. It had been a long time since I had broken into a house and not only was I rusty, but technology had moved on apace.

All three houses sported burglar alarms and no doubt an array of passive infra red boxes, tremblers, contacts - even CCTV. But that was the price of a good haul and I needed it to be good. I had no intention of doing this twice.

The house I was looking at was a semi-detached sandstone affair. A huge garden sat out back - one that had clearly been designed to allow the local second fifteen to play bounce games in it. The back was dominated by a crystal palace that the owners probably called the conservatory. It had no curtains and, as I squatted behind a compost bin, I watched the comings and goings of the owners.

As far as I could make out there were three occupants - mum, dad and teenager. Mum and dad were sitting in the glass house watching the telly and teenager had just left with his face tripping him - dad had probably told him he could only have two hundred quid pocket money this week.

I looked up and saw the light on the attic flick on. There was a dormer to front and back and I reckoned this was the teenager's room. I also had it figured that it was the way in. My guess was that neither of the dormer windows were wired up.

I decided to sit tight, wait until everyone had gone beddy byes and then make my move.

The route to the attic was easy. Or would have been had it not been for the cast on my wrist.

There was a water butt catching the rain from the conservatory (so green these people) - this would let me climb onto the edge of the conservatory, up onto the window ledge above (probably the bathroom), over to the next window and from there, to the roof and in. I had no worries that the teenager would catch me. I'd be in and out of his bedroom before he could fart.

As they say - the best laid plans.

The lights went out around the house and I waited a full hour, cold and cramp my only companions.

The night was flickering as clouds sped by - covering the moon more often than not. The next time it dropped dark I made my move.

I balanced on the water butt and hauled myself onto the top of the conservatory. Keeping my feet on the lead flashing, and away from the glass panels, I grabbed the window ledge and pulled myself up. The moon re-appeared and I froze, moving my head slowly to see if I could be spotted from any of the other houses but, even this deep in winter, the evergreen foliage was thick enough to hide the house from all around.

I prepared to move to the next ledge when a light flicked on. Framed in the window I heard the shout as the woman of the house saw my shape through the frosted glass. I tried to jump to the next ledge but my feet were poorly positioned and I felt myself slip. There was nothing to grab onto and I spun out and away from the building before crashing through the conservatory roof below.

I landed on the tiled floor in a spray of glass and the wind was kicked from my guts. I heard the start of chaos coming down stairs and tried to get up but the lack of air and the pain from my back slowed me down. Lights appeared in the hallway and I rolled onto my front. Voices shouted and I heard a man's voice tell his wife to dial the police.

I pushed up onto all fours and, as the main room behind me flooded with light, I looked for a way out.

I may have come through the roof with relative ease but the conservatory was double glazed and there was going to be no James Bond style launching myself at the glass and out into the garden beyond.

The man of the house crashed into the room and I turned to face him. He held a sawn off baseball bat in his left hand and that meant he was prepared to use force - you don't chop a baseball bat into a weapon for fun. His eyes were still watery from sleep and I had maybe thirty seconds before he was fully back on planet Earth.

I forced my lungs to grab some much needed oxygen, put my head down and tried my best Usain Bolt impression and headed for the front door. The man saw me coming and raised the bat to swing. At the last moment, I ducked and felt the rush of air as the bat parted my hair. I grabbed the door handle of the hallway door and used it to swing myself into the hall.

Like a bowling ball to the pins I took out the woman of the house as I crashed into her, phone still in her hand. She tumbled to the ground and I went with her. The scream as she went down was way too loud in my ear and the roar of the husband indicated that I was in for a serious kicking if he got to me.

I rolled over the woman and tried to get up, kicking her in the face as I scrambled for the door. She screamed again as the hall door burst open and the man took in the scene. He raised the bat and I rolled to my left as he brought it down. It bounced off the carpet and he raised it again. I lashed out with my foot and caught him on the shin. He howled and swung at my head. I ducked, but this time the bat caught me on they shoulder and it dropped numb. As he made ready to reload I stood up and charged the front door. There was a key hanging from the lock. I grabbed it and turned it.

The man brought the bat down again and I leapt towards him, ducking under the swing. I balled up my fist and sunk it into a surprisingly firm stomach. He started to double up and I used his downward momentum to thrust my head up, catching him square on the chin. He went over like a dead thing and landed on his wife. At the top of the stairs the teenager appeared. For a second I caught his eye, turned away, pulled at the front door and fled into the night.

It was a right royal fuck up but at least I could regroup and find another target.

As it was, the shitstorm was just gathering.

I jogged into the night and heard a car crank up its engine before it raced ahead of me. The doors flew open and it was goon city. I turned to escape but I was in no fit state to outrun them. I swung a fist at the first attacker but he stepped clear with ease and returned the favour to my head. I went down. A couple of kicks later and I was hauled up by the arms, and flung into the back of the car. A black cloth was placed over my head and my wrists were bound with plastic ties.

I tried to talk but a punch in my gut told me to shut up.

I was pinned between two goons. The doors were slammed shut and we took off. We didn't drive far before the car stopped and I was bundled out, onto the pavement. There was no attempt to remove the cloth or ties and I heard the doors close before the car moved off.

'Listen, shit for brains.'

The voice was loud and in my left ear. The accent was east London and the word 'brains' was accompanied by a slap to the head.

'Dupree wants you to know that you are breathing only because he feels generous. We're keeping an eye on you. Dupree wants you to walk a nice straight and narrow path. No freelancing - those days are over. Understand.'

Another slap to the head.

I nodded.

'Step out of line again and I've instructions to waste your sorry backside. So get a fucking job, save up for a mortgage and be happy that you might retire one day. Do I make myself crystal clear?'

Slap number three and four came in.

I nodded.

There was a chink of something falling on the pavement followed by the sound of fading footsteps. I waited for a few moments before trying to remove the cloth by rubbing my head on the ground. I felt something hard and cold against my cheek and I scrambled around until my hands were at the object. It felt like a Stanley knife and I carefully slid the blade out of the casing and worked it into the ties and cut them. I reached up and pulled off the cloth.

I was lying in a back street canyon of tenements. I didn't recognise the place and stood up alternately rubbing my shoulder and my face.

I got back to Martin's sometime after four and crashed.

The next morning I told him what had gone down and he called me an arsehole. I thought he was going to throw me out on the street but instead he told me that a friend of his was looking for some help in one of the big hotels in town.

'Take the job and stay clear of trouble.'

'But the photos, the account - what about Dupree?'

'It seems to me that going after Dupree is the last thing you want to do after such a warning. Take the medicine and get your head down for a while. You can always come back to him later.'

I was in no mood to let it go but with no cash, and Dupree on my case, I had little choice. If the secret to bringing the Frenchman down lay in

Mallorca then I would have to earn the money for the trip the honest way.

I agreed to the job in the hotel and Martin gave me a number to phone.

Tuesday March 18th 2008

I started the job at the hotel last night and hate it. I'm a dogsbody whose only function is to clean up everyone else's crap. I worked out that I need to stick with this job for four months to get enough cash to go to Spain. I don't think I can last four days.

Thursday March 27th 2008

Got in a fight with one of the kitchen staff. Only the intervention of Ronnie the concierge stopped me losing my job.

I'd just been to the hospital to have my cast removed and was up on the eighth floor cleaning up after a late night drunk who couldn't make it to the toilet to relieve himself. He had pissed into one of the plant pots and it had overflowed onto the tiled floor. Bucket and mop in hand I was trying to figure how to re pot the plant without touching the sodding thing when one of the kitchen crew appeared on my shoulder.

'Chef says get your arse down to the main hall. Someone has chucked up at the entrance to the kitchen and he wants it cleaned up.'

I told him to piss off. Pee I can deal with. Vomit is something else.

'Chef will be angry.'

Like I cared.

'Very angry!'

I pushed him away but he came back at me and next thing we are on the floor, rolling around, trying to knock lumps out of each other. A guest must have complained and a minute later Ronnie appeared. He grabbed us both - Ronnie is built like the QE2 - manhandled us into the service elevator and out of sight before the assistant manager appeared.

I owe Ronnie big time. He told the manager that it was two guests that had been fighting but they had run off when he appeared.

I hate this job.

Tuesday April 1st 2008

Ha, bloody, ha. The little shit that I fought with pulled an April Fool on me today. He got the head of maintenance to call me in. Technically the head of maintenance is my boss although I never really see him - mostly I'm on nights and he does days.

His name is Tam Kettering and he has been in the hotel business since birth. We've been having major problems with the plumbing on the top floor - six rooms are out of operation and the GM has been on Tam's neck to get it fixed.

What I didn't know was that they had just solved the problem and Tam was now the GM's best friend. As such he was in an unusually good mood when I rolled up.

'Ah there you are. Look, the plumbing on the top floor is still a bit dodgy and we're short of some spares. Terry (his number 2) is up to his armpits in work. Can you give the suppliers a call and order up this list? Start at the top and make it clear we need the stuff ASAP.'

He handed me a bit of paper and I was dismissed. I went into the back office and put the list on the table. They had the gig well planned and as I finished dialling Tam re-appeared. He told me to be double quick and I missed the greeting from the person on the other end.

'Hello this is the Excelsior Hotel here.' I started. 'I've been told I need to place an order for fourteen seals. It's urgent.'

There was a moment of silence on the other end of the line and then the girl asked me to repeat what I had said.

'Seals. Fourteen. It says here you'll know what type but we need them quickly.'

Too late I heard laugher from the corridor - a lot of laughter.

'Sorry sir but I'm not sure I can help. You do realise you are through to Edinburgh Zoo.'

I slammed down the phone and outside the door sounded like the audience at the funniest show on earth. I stormed out. There were at least eight in the corridor including the little shit.

Seals. Zoo. Ha, bloody, ha.

Tuesday April 29th 2008

I've been off sick for two days and thought I'd try dictating my thoughts for the first time in a while. I still hate the job but I got a bit of a promotion and no longer clean vomit and piss.

Me and the kitchen lad are still at war but he is well wary after I caught him outside a week ago and introduced his nuts to my right foot.

If I keep going at this rate I'll have enough cash to get to Mallorca by late July. The new job helps. I sometimes get front of desk and that means tips.

My guts are killing me right now. I tend to eat in the kitchen if I can and I swiped some meat from the fridge for a sandwich mid shift. If I have food poisoning I reckon I could send a bill to the hotel for the agony I have just saved them if a guest had eaten the stuff.

Martin is like a ghost at the moment. I do nights he does days. I'm gone before he is in at night and he is away before I'm back. I do weekends. He doesn't. I've seen him twice in the last few weeks and things are getting strained. I'm paying no rent and he knows I'm earning - but I can't afford to give him a penny. All I do is work, eat, shit, sleep and save.

End of recording for today. I need to go to the toilet. The meat is on its way back again.

Wednesday May 14th 2008

Back in my scratcher. This time I'm down with the flu. Martin is sick of me big time. This is the first day I can sit up. It hit me hard and I'm an invalid. I went on line this morning to check flights but I'm next to useless on the bloody thing. The prices seem to be climbing by the day - the cost of fuel has gone bananas.

Martin mentioned the 'r' word this morning and I pretended I needed to throw up. I'm not sure how much longer I can freeload.

Friday May 16th 2008

I invited the computer geek over on pain of death and he came. I asked him to do the internet thing and he came up with a package on a car, a hotel and a flight that I might just be able to afford.

He sealed the deal and I used my newly acquired debit card to pay ten percent now and the balance is due six weeks before I fly. I'll need to pull out my finger and get in the overtime if I'm to meet the bill. There is an opportunity to move to the day shift and also pull some stints behind the bar at night.

Once I'm out of this bed I'm going 24/7 to put money in the coffers and then I can get on with my real life.

Friday June the 20th 2008

I paid the balance of the trip today and I'm dead on my feet. I've never worked so hard. I haven't had a day off in over a month and I've been pulling double shifts six days out of seven. I've lost count of the times I've fallen asleep in the bar cellar or in the storage room behind the kitchen.

I've had endless stand up rows with Martin. He seems intent in making my life a misery. It all came to a head two days ago when he finally kicked me out.

I've blagged some space on Ronnie the concierge's floor for a week, but his missus is far from happy. I can think of a hundred people that either owe me a favour or I could strong arm but, if Dupree's goons are out there, they might get the wrong impression and think I was going back into business.

I'll have to work out alternative accommodation soon.

Friday June the 27th 2008

Sometimes you just need to wait and a good thing comes along. Ronnie's missus threw me out - I was two days past our agreed time and she caught me raiding the fridge for a can of lager. I had just put in an eighteen hour shift and felt entitled. She didn't see my end of the argument and my bag and coat left the third floor window of the flat. I had to sprint down the stairs before my stuff became road kill.

I wandered up to the hostel but they blanked me. I had a job and they knew it. I grabbed a bus to Martin's and was surprised that he let me in.

I had to pay up front rent but it's a quarter what I would pay outside. I've to leave his booze alone and keep the house pristine. I would also have agreed to blow off his dad if he had asked.

Martin is running hot and cold and I can't figure him from Adam at the moment.

The countdown to the trip is on but I need to get my head in gear. I need to plan my time in Mallorca. I have one week on the island and then I'm home.

I also need to call Charlie Wiggs.

Wednesday July the 2nd 2008

Charlie has arranged for me to meet his friend in Mallorca. I get the impression that the friend is a bit on the shady side and this is good news. I may need some help and an honest, upright citizen could be a dead weight.

I have the addresses of the two relevant Mallorca Security shops and my hotel is only a few streets from the shop in Inca. I've bought a map of the island and street maps for Inca and Palma. I've also entered the world of mobile communication with a 'Pay As you Go'.

My tool kit will need to be split up and put in my hold luggage. Anyone knowing what to look for could put two and two together, but I'm counting on the hold bag getting through with no checks. It's a risk I need to take. Breaking and entering is definitely on the cards and I've no guarantee I could put together a tool kit in the week that I'm in Spain.

I'll give notice that I am quitting the job next week. Hopefully they will let me work four weeks and then it's off to Espanya.

Tuesday July the 15th 2008

Something strange happened last night.

Earlier in the day I had bought a cheap, but sturdy suitcase from TJ Hughes in town and picked up a few travel essentials along with some additional clothing. I packed the clothes with the tool kit and toiletries into the new case to make sure it all fitted. I needn't have worried - I could have fitted it in twice over.

I dropped it on the floor, set up a new code on the lock and pushed it under the bed. I'll get by on the stuff I have left and I want to make sure that I can move quickly should the goons show up. I have no reason to think they will, but the closer to the flight date I get, the more I fear that something will stop me.

I went to work and came back around eight. I grabbed a glass of milk on the way up to my room and met Martin on the stairs. He looked slightly flushed and embarrassed. I asked what was up but he just shook his head, muttered something about paying your debts and squeezed past me.

I was up to date on the rent but I knew I was still a grand in the hole with him for other stuff and my promise to pay it all back within the month had been well off the mark. I entered my room, put the glass on the bedside table and slumped on the bed.

I lay for five minutes before sitting up and swinging my feet over the other side of the bed and reaching for the milk. My feet clipped the suitcase and I leaned over to push it back in. I froze.

The case had been well and truly pushed under the bed when I left. There was no doubt.

I reached down, pulled it out, placed it on the bed and checked the lock. The tell tale scratches from a knife or something sharp were scattered around the lock mechanism. I was too long in the tooth not to know when someone had been at a lock and the only person it could have been was Martin.

I dialled up the code, popped the lid and looked inside. Things looked much like I had left them. I took everything out and laid it on the bed but nothing seemed amiss. I double checked and then re-packed.

If Martin had been in the case he hadn't taken anything. But why would he want to see inside? He knew I had nothing. I thought about confronting him but if he denied it, all I could call him was a liar and that would be me back on the street.

Let sleeping dogs lie was the order of the day.

Thursday July the 24th 2008

I quit the hotel early. Too much like hard work and my mind is firmly on Spain. My boss surprised me by pulling me to one side and asking if I fancied the role as his number two. I was a slightly at a loss for words. He told me he needed someone that had both smarts and was a grafter. His current number two was retiring in three months.

I declined but I think it is the first time I've been offered a legitimate job since my days on the factory floor. I was quite touched.

I now have an outline plan of action for Spain, but it is hard to pin down exactly what I'll be doing. For a start I have three or four ideas as to how to get into the safety deposit box but I'm not even sure that there is a box - or, even if it exists that it contains anything - or if it does exist and does contain something that I will be able to get at it - or -or - or - or - you see the problem.

There is also no sign of the goons. Not even a whiff. That could be good or bad news. The good would be that Dupree considers me such a low level threat that he has reassigned his resources to better usage. The bad news is that I may now mean so little he could decide that getting rid of me might prevent a problem in the future.

I remember a lesson at school where we were discussing the Coliseum in Rome. Our teacher made the mistake of telling us that, although Nero had planned the building he had never given the famous 'thumbs down' sign in it because he died before it was completed. This opened the floodgates -

'thumbs down' - what did that mean. As soon as we found out it was a signal for the victor to kill the defeated, we were over it like a rash.

Playtime was spent 'thumbing-down' everyone in sight. That day I learned a small but valuable lesson. Even at playtime 'thumbing-down' a friend or someone you respected was far harder than 'thumbing-down' a nonentity. In fact the game showed quite a few people who their real friends were, as 'thumbing-down' often resulted in some painful punishment.

Dupree would think nothing of 'thumbing-down' me and I knew it and he probably knew that I knew and we probably both had the Kursal Flyers single 'Little Does She Know'.

Martin seems cool, if not cold but he isn't showing signs of throwing me out and, as far as I can tell, he's not been back inside my luggage.

I fly out on the 1st of August and I'm beginning to feel like a cross between a schoolboy going on his first trip abroad and someone looking at death row.

Thursday July the 31st 2008

D-day tomorrow. I need to be up with the sparrow fart but I don't care. This needs to be done. I'm not on a standard holiday package - it seems Inca isn't a hotspot for the visiting Brits - but I'm on a charter flight. Heaven help me - screaming kids, early morning boozers, cramped seating, delayed flights - the joys.

Martin is dropping me at the airport - not a happy bunny given the hour - but he'll oblige. He has been very quiet on the whole thing. I've been expecting a grilling on my plans but it hasn't happened. He knows the rough gist of the Charlie Wiggs conversation but not all of it and I'm keeping it that way.

He did ask me what the plan was when I get home and I realised I didn't have one. I've been so focused on the trip to Spain that I haven't given a second thought to what comes next. I've just assumed that whatever happens out there will dictate what happens back here. Martin was more practical. For instance where was I planning to stay? Where was the cash for living coming from? The basic stuff.

I asked if I can have one more month at his and I'll be out of his hair. As to cash, that is something I'll worry about on my return.

Early to bed.

Friday August 1st 2008

That was hell. I mean hell. Why would anyone put up with that nonsense to go on holiday? Forget the screaming kids, early boozers and delayed flights - let's talk about the woman next to me with the social graces of an ill bred monkey.

I've never hit a woman in my life but twice I had to go to the toilet - an experience in itself - to avoid assaulting her. What didn't she get about me? All I wanted to do was endure the two and half hour flight and get off the bloody plane. All she wanted to do was - and this is in rank order - chat, sing, ask me to move (three trips to the toilet), chat, borrow a pen, borrow some paper, read my newspaper, read my book, chat, fart, sing and chat - and that was all in the first hour.

She wasn't even on the pop - although she should have been on something - Valium would have been good.

Palma airport was a surprisingly cool experience - my experience of Spanish airports, albeit more than 15 years ago, revolved around planes parked on the apron and being emptied on to saunas on wheels, then standing in industrial length queues to show my passport followed by a crazy length of wait for my bags.

Instead we were offloaded through an air conditioned air bridge. The passports queue went like snow of a dyke and the bags were as quick as I could have reasonably expected.

I breathed a massive sigh of relief when my bag appeared and I wasn't stopped at customs - the tool kit had weighed on my mind for the whole flight.

Finding the car hire company was a battle. The office in the airport terminal, logically, had nothing to do with hiring cars. I was directed to a multi storey building two hundred yards away and had to dodge inbound cars and vans to find the service desk. I finally found a Spanish type queue and an hour later I was away.

Inca is not tourist central. It lies in the middle of the island and is by-passed by one of the island's few motorways. It's highly industrial and the main tourist attraction seems to be the weekly fair that runs every Wednesday. Other than that there is little to note.

My hotel is small but clean and, importantly, has the benefit of killing the climate through working air conditioning.

I dropped my bags and changed into something a little less heat retaining and went for a walk.

I found the bank quick enough and just down the road was the office of Mallorca Security. The one question still bouncing around my head is the link to the bank. The first note clearly decoded as the Colonya Caixa de Pollenca in Inca but the second sheet seems to refer to Mallorca Security. I'm working on the theory that the box, if it is a box, is in Mallorca Security and will have some connection to the bank.

I had formed the impression that Mallorca Security was a bit of a tuppence hapenny affair.

Certainly Charlie's description of the web site led me to believe that.

The truth is slightly different. The building is barely two hundred yards from the bank and looks more like a bank than the bank. It has a large frontage, which puts it at odds with the shops around it. To the left there is a shop that seems to specialise in art that is connected to light - lamp shades, chandeliers, lit sculptures - that sort of thing. It was open and a quick visit ruled it out as an entry point to my target.

The entire adjoining wall is floor to ceiling with racking, filled with every knick-knack imaginable. The wall behind looks solid concrete. There is a door at the rear to a small storage room and fortunately it was ajar. A quick glimpse inside and it was obvious the wall runs the length of the shop. If I had a jack hammer and three days to spare I might get through to the next shop.

On the other side of my target is a café and it doesn't look any more promising. This time there is no storage room, just the adjoining wall that acts as the back drop to the serving counter. It is filled with an espresso machine, a rack of various crockery and a painting of a footballer in mid scissor kick. No way through.

I wanted to get out the back and have a look at the target from the rear but it was getting late and I was tired. The last thing I needed was to get caught somewhere I shouldn't be. Anyway I need to meet Charlie's friend. For all I know the Palma branch may be a better first bet - but I doubt it.

Saturday August 2nd 2008

Charlie's friend turned out to be a bit more than ok. He is a little star. His name is David MacDonald and is one of your died in the wool ex-pats who hates everything Spanish but won't go home because of the weather.

I met him at a small café ten minutes from my hotel. He looks like he could do with a good feed. He's six feet four or so but probably weighs in at less than thirteen stone - painfully thin was a phrase created just for him.

We clicked from the start. He's big into music and we hit common ground in seconds. Him a fan of Orchestral Manoeuvres in the Dark, me a fan of Orchestral Manoeuvres in the Dark - go figure - I thought I was the only one. Fifteen minutes into the conversation he takes out a plastic folder and drops it on the table. I go to reach for it and he places his hand on it.

'Ten percent or five grand.'

I give my 'what the fuck' look and he smiles.

'The contents of the box - ten percent or five thousand - whatever is the greater.'

He had me sussed - wasn't hard. I nodded and he pushed the folder towards me. If the box turns out to have no cash I would have to worry about his five thousand later.

I opened up the wallet and pulled out a number of sheets. I realised why he had ushered me into a seat with a wall behind me. The sheets were copies of the blueprints to two buildings. Mallorca Security, Inca and Mallorca Security, Palma.

He had me well, well sussed.

I scanned them and realised things were not looking sweet.

I had expected the offices to be light weight affairs. The sheets in front of me told me that the buildings were serious about their purpose. They really were banks and banks were a completely different game. I may have been good at safes in my time but cracking a bank took a team and money - I had neither.

I sipped my coffee and flicked through the sheets.

'Not easy,' said David.

I nodded.

He reached under the table, pulled up an envelope and flicked it onto the table. I grabbed it and opened it. Inside was a blurry picture of a girl sitting at a restaurant table and scribbled below a number and a name. Her name was Maria.

'She works in the Inca branch. I think she has money problems.'

It was all he had to say about her. She was pretty although the photo wasn't good enough to make out any real detail. I took another slug of coffee. Between the plans and the girl there might just be another way to do this.

We chatted about nothing for a while and parted. I had some planning to do.

At one o'clock I was standing across from the Mallorca Security building watching the comings and goings.

The notice on the office said it was closed from half past one to five thirty - siesta time. At just after one thirty Maria emerged, locked up and headed away from me. I crossed the road and tried to keep her in sight. There was no need to play the super spy role, as she had no reason to suspect someone was watching her.

She nearly had me lost in the maze of back streets that make up the centre of the town but, at last, she stopped at a front door, took out a set of keys and then she was gone. I did a walk by. There were six flats in the block. I checked the names and there was a M Lopez Tavez. None of the rest had an M for first name. She was on the second floor.

I spent the afternoon wandering. There was nothing else to do. I hung around for an hour to see if Maria emerged but this was a non-commercial area and there were no cafés or shops to hide in. All I was doing was making myself look suspicious so I left.

At just before five I was back at Maria's door. Fifteen minutes later she emerged and I followed her back to Mallorca Security. Maria took out keys and opened up. I crossed the street and watched her through the window as she entered a code into an alarm box.

I could try and lift her keys but, from what I had seen on the blueprints, this wouldn't get me half way to where I needed to be. Anyway without the alarm code I was stuffed - given the set up it would most definitely be linked to the police - or worse.

There was no one else in the shop so I entered. I was conscious of the CCTV camera but if I was going to get Dupree I needed to take a few risks. I approached the counter and Maria smiled at me. Not half pretty.

I enquired after a security box and she responded in perfect English before handing me a small A5 flyer. It detailed the prices and the security precautions. I signed up for a box at twenty Euros a week.

To my left there was a door and I knew, from the blueprints, that both the safe and the security boxes sat behind it. On the wall next to the door was a keypad. Maria told me that when I visited I simply punch in the key number from my receipt and that would let me in to the room. She took me in to have a look.

This was way beyond the credit union set up back in Glasgow.

She entered a number on the door keypad and the door clicked. She pushed it open and we entered a room with three curtained booths. Beyond this was a second door and another keypad. She tapped in another code and led me through the door.

There was yet another door on my left and I knew that led to the safe. On my right was a bank of boxes of varying sizes. I chose one of the smaller boxes, sitting on the second row up from the ground near the far wall.

Each box had a keypad and a small handle. I was required to choose my own five digit code and set the box. I looked at my receipt and noted that my account number had five digits. Maybe the 13214 from Spencer's original sheet was both the account number and the access code - it would certainly be an easy way to remember it. Stupid but easy.

Maria stood in the room as I extracted my box. She escorted me back to the room with the booths, and told me to press the red button when I was ready to go back into the box room. She left me alone.

I took the box in to the nearest cubicle and dropped in a five euro note, closed it and pressed the red button. Maria appeared and escorted me into the box room and watched me replace the box. There was no opportunity to check out the other boxes.

Back in the main office I smiled at her.

I left and waited until she closed up at eight o'clock. No one else came to help. She seemed to run the late shift on her own. I followed her back to her flat and then I headed back to my hotel.

Sunday August 3rd 2008

Today was a dead day. The shop was closed and Maria was nowhere to be seen. In frustration I drove to Palma to look at the other Mallorca Security shop.

If anything it looks a harder nut to crack. It sits in the shadow of Palma's cathedral or as it's known 'La Seo'; a building that had its foundation stone laid in 1229, was not finished until 1601 and was still undergoing alterations as late as 1904. I have known a few builders like that in my time.

The Mallorca Security building lies on the Paseo de Born - a street dominated by a central walkway. The store is wedged between a fashion boutique and a bank. I tried to get round to the rear but as far as I could tell there seems to be no back entrance.

The day was proving to be a washout and, even though I had only been on the island three days, I was getting nervous. My flight was on Friday and come hell or high water I had to be on it.

I retired to a café and was making my nerves worse with more coffee when I caught sight of a man walking down the centre of the street. Well dressed, he had a tall slim woman hanging from his arm.

It was really the woman who caught my attention. I'm sure in Spain six feet women, dressed to kill, are the norm but even so she was a stunner. What was more intriguing was that that I knew those legs well. I caught a glimpse of the man as he turned his head to say something to her. The coffee cup in my hand froze mid air. I knew him!

I jumped up, threw a pile of Euros on the table, sprinted across the road and onto the walkway. I dropped in behind the couple and followed them as they wandered across the road and up towards the cathedral.

The stairs up to the cathedral were busy with tourists coming and going and I had to sprint the last dozen or so as my quarry turned right and out of sight. I rounded the corner into a short street that led to a square that fronted the main entrance to the cathedral. The couple jumped into one of the many horse drawn buggies that queued up outside the entrance catching the tourist euro.

I assumed they would return at some point.

The man's face played in my head. I knew it well. He was one of the two that I thought I had known from the photo back in Inca and I now knew who he was. As soon as I saw him with the long limbed beauty, two and two made four.

I had met him before and not in Spain.

On my wanderings from the hostel in Glasgow I often took a turn past a Spanish tapas bar that sat on Renfield Street. There was no way I could afford to eat there but the pair of legs that had just walked away from me in Palma, belonged to one of the waitresses in the tapas bar. It was the main reason I tortured myself with the smell of good food. I had nicknamed her Eleven - as in legs eleven - for lack of anything more imaginative.

After I moved in with Martin I discovered that the bar was one of his regular haunts. I asked if he knew Eleven. He said vaguely. That surprised me. You could hardly see those legs and vaguely remember them - not unless you were dead or not into women.

The man that I had just lost was a regular customer at the restaurant. Me in the rain, him sitting in the comfort of a dry restaurant sipping wine, chatting to Eleven and nibbling on plates of hot food. The other guy in the photo was his mate. What in the hell was Eleven doing here with one of them?

Martin is holding back. I can't believe that he hasn't seen the men in the restaurant.

I wandered for a few more hours but there was no sign of Eleven and her man. It was getting late and I gave in and drove back to Inca.

Another day gone.

Monday August 4th 2008

What a fucking day.

I waited for Maria at the shop and, when she went home for lunch, I followed her. I had made up my mind to approach her before she got back to the flat: after spending the night trying to figure a way to beat the system.

I had visited the shop twice in the morning, once when it was busy and once when it was quiet. On both occasions Maria escorted me into the box room. Short of mugging her I was at a loss as to how to check out the code from the envelope.

On the way home she stopped at a corner store. I couldn't see what she was buying but when she emerged I walked up to her and put on my best smile. She offered a polite but wary ola. I explained that I was on my way to the shop and had caught sight of her. I apologised for approaching her in the street.

'Do you fancy a cup of coffee? I have a little favour to ask.'

I expected to be blanked but she surprised me.

'There is a small café around the corner. Ten minutes and then I need to go.'

I smiled.

When we got in the café we sat at the only free table and she ordered an espresso. I doubled on that.

'So how can I help?'

'I have a small issue to do with a friend of mine,' I started. 'He is a customer of yours and, when he heard I was coming to Mallorca, he asked me to pick up something from his security box.'

'And your friend's name is…?'

'Well there it gets a little more awkward. You see the account is not his. Well not strictly his. It belongs to a friend who passed away sometime ago.'

'And their name is…?'

'Eh? Well. Awkward. My friend won't tell me but I have the code for the box.'

'So let me get this straight. A friend of yours has an account with us. Rather a friend of a friend of yours does. Your friend wants the contents and gives you the code but you don't know what this friend's friend's name is.'

I nodded.

'Senor, I cannot help you.'

'Look I know it sounds fishy but here's the bottom line. I'll give you the code. Go and check for yourself. I'm not sure the bloody thing exists. I've spent enough time on this already. I'm supposed to be on holiday.'

"So why did you open an account?"

"I wanted to check that it was possible. That's why I came in twice this morning. I mean it sounds daft to me and I wanted to check that the code I have might be genuine. My account and the friend's account numbers have the same number of digits'.

'I still cannot help.'

'Look all I'm asking for is a little help.'

'But I cannot open someone's box.'

'Why not?'

'You are not the box's owner so I cannot help.'

She drained her coffee. This was not going anywhere so I changed tack.

'Do you enjoy your job?'

'Si.'

'It seems strange that you work on your own all the time. Don't you have any help?'

'It is the way my boss likes to run things.'

'What do you do on your days off?'

She said nothing.

'You do get days off.'

She went to stand up. I reached out and put my hand on hers.

'Look I'm not an ogre and I'm not trying to chat you up. I just said I would pick up the contents for a friend and I like to keep my word.'

The chat up line was weak but to my surprise she sat back down.

'Where are you from?' I asked.

She opened up a little. Mainly small chat but she didn't seem in a hurry to get away once she got chatting.

She was from Barcelona, although she had spent ten years working in London. This explained her excellent English. She had been working in hotels. Mostly cleaning. She knew she had no future in the UK and was tired of businessmen hitting on her. It seemed that some of the guests thought that the maid was a complimentary extra. Her sister lived in Palma and had told her that a friend of her husband's was looking for someone who knew the UK, to manage one of his stores.

Maria had jumped at the chance and for a year she had managed the Palma branch of Mallorca Security.

Most of the customers were British and to her dismay the customers took it for granted she was on the game. Mallorca Security turned out to have a far sleazier clientele than even the worst hotels had exposed her to. She had complained to her boss who had moved her to the Inca branch.

Things were better in Inca. The new job was much like the old one, only quieter. At first there had been three of them working the shop but, earlier that year, this had been reduced to two and for the last three weeks she had been on her own. She worked six days a week.

'I need to go now.'

I stood up to let her leave. She looked at me.

'Come to the shop at six o'clock and I will see if I can help.'

With that she was off.

I have no idea why she changed her mind. I didn't utter a word during her monologue. Maybe she just needed someone to listen. Maybe I look sympathetic. Maybe her money problems made her act a little irrationally. Although if she had such worries she never mentioned them. I didn't care. This was the in I needed and the fact it didn't involve breaking and entering was good news.

I was outside the shop before five thirty. I wanted to check that I wasn't being set up. It had occurred to me, while lying on the hotel bed, that maybe she had decided to phone her boss and tell him about our little chat.

Two people entered and left as I looked on. Both looked like customers and, unless someone was hiding in the back shop, Maria seemed to be on her own.

I walked into the shop at six on the dot.

Maria smiled and gently nodded her head up and to the left. I put on my 'what the…' face and she did it again. I looked over and realised she was motioning towards the CCTV. I nodded and told her I wanted access to my box. She clicked the little gate that led to the box room door. I punched in my code and the door opened. I walked in.

Once inside the box room I looked round but there was no sign of a CCTV - but given the size of cameras nowadays that meant nothing. I assumed that there was none. I couldn't see anyone being too happy at being watched as they deposited and withdrew from the boxes. The few Mallorca Security customers that I had seen didn't seem the kind to take well to such intrusion.

To keep up appearances I retrieved my box and retired to one of the three small booths.

The booths looked like voting booths, even down to the small drawn curtain and shelf where you would have marked your X on the voting slip. It occurred to me that they may well be second hand voting booths - it would fit with the Mallorca Security cost ethic.

I heard the door open behind me, followed by the soft whoosh of cloth opening and a voice came from the booth next to mine.

'Give me the code.'

I told her and she left. A few seconds later and she returned, holding a box. I was surprised at how quickly she had found it. After all the only thing I had was the code and there were a lot of boxes in the room to check. I took it and laid it next to my own and lifted the lid.

My mouth dropped open.

A single sheet of paper lay in the bottom of the box. Written large in flowery script were the words:

'Bonjour. Vous êtes mort.'

I knew next to fuck all French but I recognised the word for dead. Jesus this was a set up. Either that or an elaborate joke. I closed the box and left the booth. Maria looked at me and I knew she was wondering why I didn't return the boxes to their homes. The reason was simple. If this was a set up I needed to get the fuck out of this place with speed.

As I slammed open the door leading to the front shop I saw two men standing at the entrance door. Both were looking directly at me. As soon as I appeared they stepped forward. I weighed up the option to charge them, but they were bruisers and focussed on me. Dupree's men. I jumped back into the room and pulled the door shut. I heard the lock click and could only hope they didn't have the access code. I turned to Maria.

'Is there another way out?'

'Why?'

'There are two men about to break down that door and they don't want to talk to me about the weather.'

She surprised me by running past me towards the door. I thought she was going to open it. Instead, she slammed her hand on a small red button on the wall. I heard a click and then an alarm went off.

'They won't be able to get in. The alarm changes the code.'

'How do we get out?'

'We don't. We wait on the police.'

'The police. I don't want the police.'

'What else would you have me do?'

She tilted her head towards the ceiling.

I looked up and spotted a tiny camera - almost hidden from view. I realised that I had gone into thick mode. She was acting exactly as she should have in the situation.

A customer had just told her he was under attack and she had hit the alarm. If someone was recording this, then her actions wouldn't look out of place; she was one smart cookie.

I had no choice but to wait for the police to arrive, and they did within minutes. I heard rapping on the door and a splash of Spanish. Maria responded and unlocked the door.

Two policemen stood in the doorway. Maria went all talk, talk, talk and I was ushered out of the room. Once they had established I couldn't speak Spanish one of them told me, in broken English, to sit on a chair. When they were finished with Maria she came over with them and acted as translator.

'Just tell them what happened,' she said.

I kept it simple and didn't embellish. I told them that I had seen the two men advance towards me and panicked. They asked if I had any reason to think they would attack me. I told them that I didn't. The questioning turned to who I was, where I was staying and so on. The conversation was shorter than I expected and, after a few minutes more with Maria on her own, they left.

'You should go now. My boss will be here. The alarm goes to his mobile phone.'

She was whispering. Christ the place was bugged for sound as well.

'Will he know you let me see the other box?' I whispered back.

'I will quit before he finds this out. Now go.'

I got up and, with a thank-you, I left.

Outside I scanned the road and pavements. I was certain that the two men would be waiting. It was just a matter of where.

I headed away from my hotel. My head was in a flat spin. None of this made sense. Why would Dupree set me up? Why had the men not lifted me before I went to the shop? It was hardly the best place to grab someone. Had Dupree conned Martin and Spencer into helping or had he threatened them? If so, to what end? Why the hell lead me to Spain? More questions than answers.

I turned into the first street and then left into the next. The road headed up a hill and under a bridge. I walked quickly and as I passed under the bridge I looked back and saw the two men less than fifty yards behind me. I hit the gas pedal and sprinted up the incline.

At the top, the street opened into a wide boulevard peppered with shops. There were some shoppers around but probably not enough to worry my pursuers.

I ran across the boulevard and saw a small lane on my left. It was roofed in and I dived into it -

hoping it wasn't a dead end. I slowed to a jog - there was no way I could keep a sprint on. Then I had an idea. Not a good one, but an idea.

I exited onto another road and turned in the direction of my hotel. I checked behind and the two men tumbled out behind me. I moved back to a jog.

After a couple of hundred yards I slowed to a quick walk as I was running out of breath again. A glance behind and the two men were also walking. At the next corner I walked out of view and then, grabbing energy from somewhere, I ran, sprinted for thirty yards and dived into a small gap between a house and a factory.

There was a wall about five feet high at the end of the gap and I jumped over it and into a small courtyard. A quick scan and I could see there was no way out, save through a series of what looked like back doors.

I slumped behind the wall, counted to thirty and then looked back over the wall. I could see maybe two yards of pavement from where I was and there was no sign of the pursuers. I jumped back into the small alley and slowly walked up to where the pavement started.

I poked my head around and looked to the left. About twenty yards away the two men were gazing around, one of them was on the phone - I ducked back in. I waited for another count of thirty and looked out. The men were gone. I exited the gap and ran to my right and hit the road that the hotel lay in.

If there were others waiting at my hotel I was screwed but there was fuck all I could do about that.

I hit the lobby at a flat spin and raced up the stairs to my room. Two minutes later and I was back on the street, suitcase in hand. I thanked God that I had kept it packed and ready to go.

I pulled the car keys from my pocket. The car was parked at the end of the hotel road and, as I jumped in, I heard a shout. I slammed the door shut and hit the central locking before pushing the key into the ignition. My hands were sweating but I got the key home first time and started the engine. I heard a thump as someone or something hit the car and I hit the accelerator. I glanced in my rear view mirror and saw the two men screaming at me.

I kept my foot down and horns went up around me before I realised I was driving on the wrong side of the road. I came within inches of front ending a Fiat 500. I swerved to the right and spent ten minutes losing myself in the maze of streets before heading for the motorway that led to Palma.

I had no plan beyond getting the hell out of Inca and, as I passed a Lidl supermarket I hit a roundabout that sat above the motorway. I only had eyes for Palma and the plane home. But the flight was four days away. Add to this that Dupree would have a watch put on the airport and I changed my mind and took the motorway north to Alcudia and Puerto Pollensa.

I kept my foot as close to illegal as made no difference - putting the miles between me and Inca. At the Puerto Pollensa turnoff I slid off the motorway and turned left towards Pollenca and Puerto Pollensa.

Five miles along the road I pulled off onto a dirt track. The light had long since gone and the adrenalin from the encounter had turned sour. I found an open gate to a field and slid the car into the field.

I put my head back and dozed for an hour before waking and pulling out my digital recorder to waffle for a while.

It's time for bed and I have no plan for tomorrow.

Tuesday August 5th 2008

I was woken this morning by an irate farmer leaning on the horn of his tractor. He was sitting in the lane with a face like fizz. I got my shit together and pulled out of the field and headed back for the main road. With no better idea of what to do next I hung a right and pointed the car towards Puerto Pollensa.

The road was quiet and my mind wandered as I sped along. I hit a small industrial area and entered Puerto Pollensa via a roundabout that had a Fairview yacht franchise on one corner and an Eronski supermarket on the other. The town closed in around me and a few hundred yards later I reached the sea front.

Puerto Pollensa is essentially a holiday destination mixed in with a high number of ex Pats working their way to a funeral in the sun. The town is small and compact. The centre is a small maze of three and four storey canyons. I cruised around and exited the town onto what looked like a new ring road. I followed it round the town and crossed where I had come in. I kept going and dropped down to the beach front.

The beach was quiet and well ordered - none of your Magaluf or Palma Nova nonsense here. There are no towering hotel blocks lining the sea front. In fact it is more akin to a quiet US gulf coast town than your typical Spanish resort of old.

I parked the car across from the beach and got out. A small wall separated the sand from the road and a tractor was towing a rake behind it bringing order to the area. I sat on the wall and stared at the sea.

To my left a marina harboured a range of small yachts. To my right the coast disappeared into the distance.

Puerto Pollensa sits in a small bay and I looked over at the rocky promontory that formed the far side. Out on the bay a small fishing boat was setting out for sea and I wished I was on it.

The idea of being on the boat took on merit as I watched it carve a route through mirror calm waters. I could wait until Friday and try and exit through Palma airport but the odds seemed stacked against that being a trouble free journey. The alternative was staring me in the face.

Mallorca is the northern most island in the Balearics and there is clear sea between it and the coast of Spain. Not only that but it lies less than 200 kilometres from Barcelona. I figured that there must be some traffic between the two. Not the commercial ferry type - that might be being watched - but more the casual tourist type. Surely someone in the marina might be heading for Barcelona at this time of year.

Once in Barcelona I would head for Girona airport to the north. From there to Prestwick Airport in Scotland on a cheap Ryanair flight. That way I would exit Mallorca without going via Palma and enter Scotland without visiting Glasgow Airport. At least I would give myself a chance to get home without Dupree finding me.

It sounded good but I had no idea how difficult it would be to find someone that was both going to

Barcelona, and willing to take a stranger. I went back to the car and drove to the town centre. Once I had parked up I walked down to the marina, picked a bar that overlooked the complex and ordered a coffee.

It was still early and people were thin on the ground. I was close to the entrance to the marina and watched the comings and goings.

An hour later, a little hotter and none the wiser I was still sitting in the same chair. I ordered a Coke.

I simply had no idea where to start. How do you hitch a lift in a boat?

The morning meandered along and I considered and reconsidered my options. Lunchtime arrived and the café busied up. I hadn't eaten since yesterday afternoon and I ordered pizza and a large plate of chips along with another Coke.

As I ate, I studied the other patrons hoping for some divine inspiration.

By two o'clock I was getting depressed. The lack of action was killing me.

At the back of my head I had the nagging feeling that the goons from Inca wouldn't take long to figure where I was. After all how hard could it be?

I got off my seat and went for another wander and, as I walked, I passed a small bar ringing with laughter and looked in. Four men were standing at the bar giving the local beer a good hiding. I walked up to the bar and ordered a pint of what they were downing and earwigged the conversation, letting the alcohol take the edge off my growing frustration.

It became clear that the men owned a yacht in the marina and were on holiday. In for a penny and in for a pound, I gate crashed their conversation and asked which boat was theirs?

They were unfazed with my interruption and one of the men nodded to the door and we walked over. He pointed to the marina and tried to guide my eye to their boat. I couldn't swear that I was looking at the right one but when I asked what type it was he went off on one. Halfway through I had to own up to knowing nothing about boats, but this just made him more vocal on the subject.

We drifted back to his mates and I bought a round. This went down well and soon I was knee deep in nautical terms and stories.

The guys were good company. They had been friends since school and acted the way you do when you know someone so well that you can read their thoughts. Ten years ago they had agreed to buy a quarter each of a yacht. None of them knew the first thing about sailing but they all fancied it. The current yacht was their third and a source of pride and joy.

I asked where they had been and where they were heading.

'Malaga then San Antonio in Ibiza then Mahon in Minorca and we came in here two days ago. If things go well we want to try and get to Barcelona and then down the coast and back to Malaga.'

I was amazed they didn't notice my double take when they said Barcelona.

'When do you head off?'

The guy who had tried to show me the boat told me they were leaving first thing in the morning. They wanted to try and get there while it was still light. I asked if they wanted a passenger and they laughed. I said I was serious and they went cold on me. Then they got bored with me and made their excuses before leaving.

I sat with my drink and contemplated my next move.

I could trawl the marina for someone else bound for Barcelona but I could look long enough.

I left the bar and found the four men a couple of bars away. I didn't go in but found a cafe opposite and waited.

Just after four they tumbled out and walked towards the marina. I fell in behind them, keeping well back. They were laughing and joking as they staggered out onto one of the piers. Four boats from the end they leapt on board a tidy looking motor cruiser. I reckoned she was forty feet, maybe a bit more, in length. I retreated to the entrance of the marina and decided on a course of action.

I returned to my car and emptied the suitcase onto the back seat. Bundling a few toiletries and one change of clothes into the front seat, I packed the rest into the boot and closed it. A trip to a nearby Spar and I had purchased two two litre bottles of water, a large bag of crisps and four chocolate bars. I asked the shopkeeper for an extra plastic bag and I bundled the stuff on the front seat into the spare bag.

A few moments later and I drove the car to a public car park, locked it and placed the keys behind the front left wheel. Avis would find out about it when I got home.

I chose another café that faced the marina and settled in for the wait.

Just before seven I saw the four men making their way to the town. The laughing and joking had been replaced by silence as the alcohol in their system took its payment for the early jollity it had provided. As they walked past I dropped my head under the table, as if I was looking for something.

Once they were gone I got up and walked into the marina.

It was dark but there were signs of life everywhere and I nodded to a few people as I worked my way out to the boat - trying to look as if I belonged there.

Luckily there was no one else on the nearby boats and I slipped on board the four lads' cruiser, clutching my two bags.

I had expected the door to the cabin to be locked, and already had my hands on my tool kit, but it was open and I went inside. I entered a living room with bench seats down either side. A small kitchen was tucked into the left hand corner near the entrance. To the right was a small toilet. At the far end there were two doors. Both opened onto bedrooms. The one on the left was the master bedroom with a large double bed. The one on the right was smaller with two single beds against each wall - barely inches between them. I wondered who shared the double bed?

Returning to the deck I scanned the rest of the boat. Two chairs sat either side of the door to the cabin, one with the steering wheel and various instruments in front of it.

Behind the chairs sat a horseshoe arrangement of two long runs of plastic covered seating with a gap at the rear for the entrance to the boat. In the centre of the horseshoe the floor shone with wooden decking. A large trapdoor sat near the back and when I lifted it I found myself looking down on the engine. I closed it and went back to the cabin but after a few minutes I realised there was nowhere to hide.

Back on the deck I reopened the trap door to the engine room and dropped in.

I had to bend double due to the low roof.

The room was dominated by the engine but it was possible to circle it. I did so and, at the back sat a row of cupboards. A quick search of the cupboards revealed an array of bits and bobs from rope to torches. Below them was a door that ran the width of the boat. The door opened by dropping to the floor. Inside was a dog's dinner of material including what looked like a lifetime's supply of porn.

I bent down and realised that if I pushed everything to the front I could slip in behind the contents and hide. I wouldn't survive a military inspection but nothing in the cupboard looked like it was well used - save the magazines. I didn't think that the men would be back for a while so I re-arranged the cubbyhole to leave a space at the back.

Happy that I could slip in quickly, I exited the engine room, jumped off the boat and returned to the town.

It took me half an hour to find the men. They were sitting in a restaurant chatting quietly, water not booze stood on the table and it was obvious they were keeping a clear head for the morning.

At ten thirty they waved for the bill and I made my move. I walked quickly back to their boat, jumped on board and opened the engine room door. I dropped down and pulled it shut.

The place was pitch black and I cursed myself for not bringing a torch. I banged both shins getting to the cupboard, cut my thumb fiddling with the latch and settling in took longer than I had expected. I heard the sound of footsteps on the boat just as I pulled the cubby hole door shut.

There was a lot of clumping and chat as the men readied for bed. I soon discovered that my head was below the toilet, as one of the men dropped a log that sent a nightmare smell into my space.

After an hour the boat fell quiet and I realised that I should have stayed on the dock and snuck in later. It was already getting cramped and hot but I couldn't risk moving around. If someone heard any noise it wouldn't take long to find me.

I tried to make myself comfortable but I was on a loser. Twisting and turning, all in silent mode, I put my hand on the familiar tube of a torch. I pulled it to my body, covered the lens and threw the switch. At least I had light. I didn't think it would be seen upstairs. I hoped it wouldn't be seen upstairs.

So here I lie whispering into the recorder.

I have no idea what tomorrow might bring.

Wednesday August 6th 2008

Hell. It is a simple as that. Hell. To say I am relieved to be on dry land and out of the boat is the understatement of my life.

Around seven o'clock this morning there were signs of life above. I was already in a bad place. Cramped and unable to go for a piss I had eventually emptied one of my bottles, mostly on the floor and re-filled it with urine. It was a not my finest moment but at least it was better than pissing in my trousers. Not than anyone would have noticed the smell if I had - every time any one used the toilet I got the full bhoona. I have no idea what the men were eating last night but it wasn't a light salad.

The engine kicked into life just before seven thirty and I realised that what I thought was a crap idea took a shovel and dug deep. The noise from the engine, and it was still only on tick over, was deafening. The diesel power plant lay less than three feet from my head and the combination of the noise and vibration blocked out the world. When the engine note deepened there was a slight swaying, and I realised we were moving.

Ten minutes later the driver turned the engine up to eleven and my life became a maelstrom of noise and motion. The boat planed and I rolled towards the cubby hole door. The nose would dip to bite through a wave and I would roll to the front of the boat. Then the boat would lift clear and I would roll back - this process went on endlessly.

As we broke from the bay the current or the waves or some act of nature worked on the side of the boat and gave the up and down motion a side to side lilt. Every so often we would hit a larger than normal wave and my head would be slammed off the roof of the cubby hole.

I was forced to grab a rope coil and wrap it around my head like a Sikh's turban. It was uncomfortable but gave me some protection against the wave movement. It also dulled the noise a little, but not much. I rearranged the angle I lay at and tried to wedge myself in a way that would reduce the rolling.

I realised that I lacked one vital piece of information that might have made the whole thing bearable. How long would this go on? I had no real idea of what the distance from Mallorca to Barcelona meant in terms of nautical time. The only information I had to go on was the discussion with the men when they said they wanted to get the trip done in daylight. Dusk was twelve hours away and I tried to settle down and ride it out.

Two hours into the journey and I was on the verge of giving up and handing myself in. It was unbearable. Even if they decided to turn back and drop me in Mallorca it had to be better than this.

The throbbing of the engine had hard-wired a headache of growing proportions into my skull. The rope around my head kept slipping off and was chafing my skin. The air was burning hot. The combination of the rising temperature outside and the heat of the engine had driven the atmosphere in the engine room to well beyond something I could survive long.

I opened the cubby hole door and rolled out into the engine room. The noise rose another notch and I crawled round to the hatchway. I was reaching up to push the hatch open when a breath of cool air brushed my wrist. Moving my arm around in the dark I picked up the draught and followed it back to its source. I felt a handle above me and the draught was coming from just beneath it. I crawled back to the cubby hole to get the torch.

Back at the handle I flipped on the light. No one would notice it up top in broad daylight. There was a small door about three feet by three feet in front of me. On my initial recce of the room I had missed it. I pulled on the handle and the door opened outwards and I was washed with cool air. I gulped it in like water to a man in the desert.

The space beyond was empty and, at the back there was another small hatch. Sunlight shone from beyond and it was through this gap that the air was coming.

I pulled myself up and into the small space, reached out and grasped the hatch. I pushed it and it started to fall away. I caught it before it fell open and crawled a bit further into the space, grateful for the cool air.

Beneath me was a metal walkway - ridged to prevent slipping and bordered with two small metal edges about an inch proud of the surface, running the length of both sides. It was a gangplank. I'd seen a few in the bigger boats at the marina. They slipped out of the rear of the boats like tongues to form a bridge between the marina pontoons and the boat.

The boat I was on had been side into the pontoon and the gangplank had been stored. I felt along the underside of the gangplank and realised that it was telescopic. My feet were hanging out into the engine room and my face was inches from the hatch.

The cool draft was being drawn in by the wake of the boat. As the boat progressed the rear caused a minor vacuum and air rushed in to fill it. The only down side was that occasionally the exhaust from the engines would get caught in the vacuum and pour into the space. But, compared to the hell-hole I had been in, this was sweet.

I wanted to pop the hatch to let more air in but anyone sitting at the back of the boat might see the door open and wonder why. I risked cracking it a little more and this increased the flow of fresh air.

If someone opened the engine room hatch my feet would be in plain sight, but there was fuck all I could do about this. I could curl up for a little while but the space was too small to stay that way for long. Anyway all I could hope was that the more miles we put between boat and Mallorca, the less likelihood that they would turn back if I was found.

I must have dozed off at some point because I was woken by the noise of the engine note dropping. The engine was kicked into idle and immediately the movement of the boat took on a much more unstable wobble. I wondered if we were at our destination but it seemed too soon.

There were voices above me but the engines had set up a ringing in my ears that made it impossible to make out what they were saying.

It reminded me of the time when I was twelve years old and had sneaked into the Apollo in Glasgow to watch Deep Purple. The ringing in my ears had lasted three days. I reckoned that by the time I got to Barcelona the ringing would still be going at Christmas.

With the boat now still, the flow of fresh air stopped and the gangplank space soon took on the temperature of the engine room. The rocking continued which suggested we were not moored up and when I caught the clink of glasses I figured they had stopped for lunch.

My throat was dry and the 2 litre bottle of water had long since gone. I reached for the little hatch and cracked it a little more and pushed my head into the gap. It wasn't much cooler but it was better than nothing.

Forty minutes crawled by and I was on the point of giving up again when the engine fired up and we lurched forward. The movement caught me by surprise and I let go of the hatch. It fell away - banging against the hull. I froze, waiting for someone to notice, but nothing happened. I tried to reach out and pull the hatch closed but I would have needed to lean my head and shoulders out to reach it, and that was asking for trouble. I left it alone.

The air flowed freely, now joined by salt spray. I could see the Mediterranean framed where the hatch door had been. There was no sign of land.

An hour later a large black and white ship slid across my little picture frame. The words Barcelona-Mahon were writ large on the side. I smiled. At least we were on the main ferry route and this suggested that we were still on track for Barcelona.

Around five o'clock the engine dropped its note again. In the last hour I had seen an increasing number of boats and ships that suggested we were getting closer to land. Pulling myself forward I risked poking the top of my head out and was rewarded with the sight of the rising cliff that sat above the commercial port of Barcelona. I knew that on top of the cliff sat the Parc de Montjuic and just out of sight was the old Olympic Stadium.

The boat purred along parallel to the shore, keeping the commercial port on her left until we reached the entrance to the main marina. I wriggled back into the engine room and felt a wall of heat wash over me. Closing up the door to the gangplank, I crawled around the engine and back into my cubby hole.

The boat seemed to take an age before the engine was killed and the guys upstairs stopped moving around and got off. I waited for another ten minutes to make sure they were gone and crawled back through the engine room before opening the main hatch. For the first time in nearly twenty hours I stood up and felt my back crack. The boat was deserted and I wasted no time getting off the bloody thing.

I got my bearings and headed for the exit from the marina.

Half an hour later, and a full two litres of Coke in my stomach, I was in a public toilet at the bottom of Las Ramblas. My face in the mirror was black with diesel smoke and I was sporting the kind of hair that you get by plugging your fingers into the mains.

Stripping to my waist I did the best I could to clean my hair, face and arms. I scrubbed out my armpits and retired to a cubicle and slipped out of the rest of the clothes and put on the spare stuff from the plastic bag. I bundled the soiled clothes into the bag and 'over skooshed' some deodorant on all offending parts.

Back at the sink I brushed my teeth and straightened myself up.

I walked out into the evening and found Las Ramblas rammed with tourists and pretty people going for a walk.

The place was alive. Chatting, drinking and eating were the norm as I wandered up and away from the sea. I passed a row of living statues, all of them impressively made up.

One, a small evil looking dwarf had painted his entire body, including his tongue, green and delighted in slobbering and gibbering at tourists who approached him. No one dared go near him and I wondered how he made any money as the statues relied on tourists filling the plates or hats that sat in front of them.

I turned into the gothic quarter, made my way to a small internet café and found a terminal. Ordering up three cokes and a coffee I added a spectacularly sticky bun and the waiter looked at me with a look that said 'you greedy bastard'.

I pulled up the Ryanair site and after a major struggle booked the last flight out of Girona that night at an exorbitant price. By my reckoning I had three hours to make the flight.

I killed the cokes and the coffee and wolfed down the bun before heading back into the night. I walked up Las Ramblas to the square at the top and over to El Corte Inglis, Spain's' answer to Debenhams, and jumped in one of the taxis sitting there. The driver's face lit up when I said Girona. I asked how much and he said a hundred Euros. I winced but nodded my head, and we were away.

The taxi drive took over an hour and I was dropped at a building site that doubled as an airport. The place was tourist city but I put on my patient head and joined the queue for my plane.

I'm sitting in the middle of a row of three seats, with a snoring man who keeps trying to use my left shoulder as a pillow, and a woman who has drunk herself into a stupor on my right. Around me the plane is quiet and the lights low.

Bring on tomorrow.

Thursday August 7th 2008

I got in late last night. I assumed Martin was in bed and I didn't wake him. When I got up in the morning he was gone. I wasn't actually sure if he had been in. A quick peek in his room and it didn't look slept in. Then again he was neat and probably made the bed up before he left. As I yack into this thing, there is still no sign of him and it has gone ten o'clock at night.

The day has been a quiet one. I went over the events in Mallorca until I was blue in the face but I can't make head nor tail of them. The whole thing was a set up. Of that there is no doubt, but the question is why and why in that manner?

If Dupree has decided I am excess baggage then he could have taken me down long ago. I have one working theory, and it is a poor one at best.

I'm thinking that Dupree knew of Spencer's intentions and also found out about the box in Mallorca. He could have raided it, removed anything that might incriminate him and have left the single sheet of paper for anyone else that came along. When someone was fool enough to appear, then the local goon squad were alerted and that was why I was caught bang to rights in the shop.

As such there may be no pre-meditation in all of this. I simply followed the trail that someone else had already trodden. What I can't figure is how they knew I was in the shop at that particular moment. Maria might have been in on it and the whole 'helping me' thing was a game. It would certainly explain the ease with which she decided to lend me a hand. But then why hit the alarm and save me? If she was in on it she could have just left me to the goon patrol. So if she didn't alert them then who did and why?

I haven't got any answers to this one yet. I'll front up with Martin when he gets back and see if he has any ideas.

Sunday August 10th 2008

No sign of Martin. When he was still A.W.O.L. on Friday I put it down to him going away for the evening and not informing me. However he should have been back Friday night as a minimum, as he was picking me up from the return flight. I fully expected him to appear on Friday evening in a rage, having driven out to Glasgow airport only to discover I wasn't on the plane.

I've tried his mobile but it isn't even tripping to answer machine. It simply rings out and then dies. On Saturday I tried a few of his usual haunts but with no success. I didn't push too hard. If Dupree wants me I'm not going to spread myself around town and advertise my whereabouts. I'm assuming that Martin's house is safe, if for no other reason than that I would be dead by now if Dupree wanted me and knew I was holed up with Martin.

Mallorca is still spinning in my head but I'm no further forward.

Monday August 11th 2008

They found me. It was gone midnight last night and I was watching 'A Tree Grows in Brooklyn' on TCM - a weepie but a good one. I heard the door handle being turned and expected Martin to walk in, but when I saw the goon patrol from Mallorca bowl into the room I knew I was in a world of trouble.

Fortunately I hadn't been on the giggle juice and my head was clear. They rolled in and I rolled off the settee and leapt to my feet. They headed for me but I was into the kitchen and out the back door like a cat with a poker up its arse. They gave chase but it was dark and I simply sprinted into the field behind Martin's house and circled back on myself. I lay flat as the goon patrol squelched around for ten minutes and left.

I was in no position to move on. I needed my stuff from the house.

I sat for an hour in the chill and then approached the back of the house. There was no sound from within and I clambered onto the roof of the old coal hut with all the grace of a cat fifteen years past its prime.

My bedroom window sits above the hut and the latch on the window gave easily to a penknife. I climbed through the window and gathered up my stuff. Bag packed I went to the bedroom door and listened. If I was going to be out on the street for the night I could do with my jacket and some food. Both were downstairs.

I listened and I could hear the TV still playing out the end of the movie but nothing else. If the goons were in the house then they were playing it quiet.

I opened the bedroom door a touch and slipped out onto the small landing. The stairs in front of me dropped straight down to the front door. The first three steps were hidden from view but after that you could be seen from the living room.

I bent down and placed my hands on the first step and leant forward. The bit of the room I could see looked empty. I pushed my head a little further until the fireplace came into view and there was still no sign of life. Dropping my right hand one more stair I leant down and took in most of the rest of the room. Empty.

I stood up, grabbed a lungful of air and walked down the stairs. The front door was frosted glass but you could still see shapes through it and I tried my best to avoid it by leaping from the middle of the staircase straight into the room. As I landed I froze, waiting for an attack from either the kitchen or the front door. Nothing happened and I crossed to the kitchen door. The light was off and in the dark I loaded up on chocolate, crisps and diet Irn Bru.

I walked back into the living room and eyed my jacket hanging on a coat peg next to the front door. If anyone was watching then my shadow would be a give away. I walked to the stairs and dropped to my knees, then to my belly and wriggled towards the front door. If someone came in now I was a goner.

I reached the door and slid up the wall until I could relieve the coat peg of my jacket, caught it as it fell and wriggled back to the stairs.

I was half way up the stairs when the front door opened with a vengeance and the goons reappeared. Common sense would have been to lock it but it had never occurred to me.

I flew up the remaining steps, ran into my bedroom, slammed the door behind me, picked up my bag and scrambled through the open window. The door to the bedroom bounced off the wall behind me as the goon patrol entered at high speed.

I was on the coal hut roof and, with a leap, I dropped to the concrete below. Above me one of them shouted but I was over the fence and back into the field - this time I didn't double back I just kept running.

As my breath shortened I began to ease up and turned sharp left. In the far distance I could see the main road through the village of Eaglesham. Behind me there was another shout but it was too far away to be an issue. I made for the light.

The trek was tough - crossing fields in the dark is not easy and I had no light to see by. After an hour I reached the village but stopped short of entering the pool of light that the street lights cast.

I had no idea where I was heading but it needed to be away from here. The goon patrol would not give in easily. Dupree was a bastard of the first order and failure was not tolerated well. The fact that they had been given a second chance and sent in after their failure in Spain was surprising enough.

I skirted the road and made my way through another field - keeping the road to my right. Twice I had to divert to avoid houses and then I hit a stretch of homes running across my path. I picked the one with the lowest fence and jogged through the garden and out onto the road on the other side.

The main road was to my left and knew if I turned right there was the Chinese restaurant on one side and the row of shops, a little further down, on the other side. At this time they would all be shut. Turning right would lead me into an estate and, much as I wanted to play hide and seek with the goon patrol, I needed to put distance between the village and me.

I had a local taxi number on my mobile and I gave them a call before dipping back behind the house to wait.

Ten minutes later a car turned up and I walked out as if I had just left the back door. If the driver knew the occupants he didn't ask or couldn't care. I told him to head for Glasgow and I sat back to think.

I had no place to go. No one to turn to. Martin's disappearance could mean that Dupree had found out he was harbouring me and that was that for Mr Sketchmore. The hostel was a maybe until I realised that there might be a second goon patrol waiting for me at my old haunt.

The car cruised into the outskirts of the city and the driver asked where in Glasgow.

'The Gorbals.'

I told the driver the street I wanted and I wasn't even sure that it still existed. The car soon swung into the road and, to my amazement, familiar tenements sprang up on both sides. I showed the taxi driver which close to stop at and paid him from my ever-dwindling supply of cash.

Standing on the pavement, bag in hand, I realised this was the long shot of all long shots but desperate people do desperate things.

I walked into the close, climbed the stairs to the second floor and stood in front of a large storm door. There was no nameplate. I rang the bell and waited. I was about to hit it for the second time when I heard movement inside.

The inner door opened and the left hand storm door pulled back an inch. I waved sheepishly at the crack and the door closed. A second later and the sound of bolts being withdrawn scraped around the landing. The door opened and a woman in a badly fitting dressing gown looked out.

'Hi Rachel.'

'Fuck.'

The awkwardness stretched for a while before she stepped back and let me in. She looked good, better than she had when I last saw her in the prison visiting room. I wondered if she thought the same about me.

'I take it you want a bed?'

I nodded and she opened the first door on the left.

'In there! We'll talk in the morning. I need my sleep. I have to work.'

With that she closed the door and left me. I looked at the room. Well kept. A single bed. Nice carpet. Fresh wallpaper and the various bits and bobs around the place suggested that Rachel wasn't scraping by.

I kicked off my clothes, dropped them in a bundle next to my bag and slipped into the bed.

I hated using the digital recorder at first and I've no idea why I keep doing it. I don't expect anyone to listen to it but I don't care. Somehow it seems to keep things in order despite the craziness around me. Sometimes I just whizz the thing back to a conversation I recorded or a little rant from myself and find a little oasis at the end of the day - when I'm in the mood. An oasis that lets me mull over my life in bite sized chunks.

It's also useful to flick back through time and get a sense of proportion over circumstances. It's anything but neat and at times sounds like someone spinning an FM dial and recording the output. But it is important to me.

My life is a long way from where I expected it to be at my age. My prospects are shot. I'm a wanted man on the run with little or no one to turn to and I have no resources to fall back on. I thought the low points in my life were the first day in prison or the first day in the hostel. I was wrong. This is far worse.

At least in prison I had some sort of future. Bide my time and I would get out. In the hostel I had the same feeling but now I can't see the future. I can't see a way out of this. I can see my death and somehow that seems less important than it should. The alternative is living in fear. Forever on the run. Begging for food. Sleeping rough.

Maybe I could get back on my feet but would Dupree let me?

Surely he would be waiting, a spectre waiting in the shadows. What kind of life would that be? Maybe death is not such a bad option.

Maybe?

Tuesday August 12th 2008

The conversation with Rachel started as well as could be expected. It was shit. I mean what did I expect? Apart from the brief meeting in prison, when she handed me the letter, I'd had no contact with her from the day I crapped on her and Martin. She had said nothing during the meet in prison but she had plenty to say this morning.

I woke up to the smell of cigarette smoke. I dressed and followed the trail to the living room. Like the bedroom it was neat, tidy and well furnished.

Rachel sat at a small table next to the main window with a cup of coffee in front of her and a ciggie hanging from her left hand. She was dressed in a neat two piece suit with a crisp white blouse and a pair of smart dark shoes with a low heel. The skirt showed off enough leg to tell me she was keeping herself in shape.

She looked up when I entered.

'I leave for work in half an hour,' she said. 'This had better be good.'

I hadn't planned this conversation and I felt at a loss. Should I tell her everything, nothing or something? Could I trust her? I started by giving her a little potted history about me since prison but she cut me off.

'Stow it. Martin's told me it all.'

Now that was a revelation. Martin hadn't mentioned Rachel since we met up again. I assumed it was over, but clearly it wasn't.

'He says you're trouble.'

Thanks Martin.

'I can only assume you're here because he's thrown you out. So I'll tell it as it is and then you leave.'

She took another drag.

'I'm doing ok. I'm off the game and have been for nearly two years. I've got a nice little job as a sales rep for a lingerie firm. I've put enough cash away to own this place and I don't need any shite in my life. So here is how it is going to go down. When I leave you leave. You move on and don't come back. I ain't scared of you anymore. Martin has told me where you're at in life and I can't say I'm sorry. You caused a lot of pain, and hurt a lot of people. In my view God is getting even with you. So I don't expect to see you again. If I do, I make a call to the police and tell them you are stalking me.

Is that clear? Crystal clear?'

Not much you can say to that really. I nodded and opened my mouth to say something. She didn't let me get a word out.

'I'm not giving you any cash. So don't ask.'

Psychic or what.

'Pack up your stuff and go.'

I couldn't think of anything to say. So I didn't and went back to the bedroom to pack up. A wash and brush up in the neat and tidy toilet and I was ready to go. The problem was where?

I had a thought and went back to see Rachel.

'When did you last see Martin?'

'None of your business - now shift.'

'Only,' I went on, 'I haven't seen him since Thursday. He hasn't been back at his house.'

She looked away and reached for another cigarette.

'I haven't seen him since Monday. He phoned Tuesday night but he was in a bad mood.'

'I got back mid week.' I avoided saying from where. 'He could have been out when I got in but he certainly hasn't been there since.'

She sat down and lit up.

'Martin's been uptight for months now. A real pain in the tits!'

Rachel picked up her mobile from the mantelpiece and hit a few buttons.

'Answer machine' she said after a few seconds. 'No point leaving a message. He never returns the call.'

It occurred to me that Martin had more than one mobile. The number I had didn't have an answer machine. The clock chimed the half hour and I expected Rachel to move but she sat, drawing in the smoke, staring at the window.

'What made you come back?' she asked.

'Where else would I go? You know the hole I'm in.'

'Kind of. Martin said you're in the mire with some French boy. Is that true?'

'In a way.'

'So what will you do now?'

'Back to the hostel and see if they will give me a bed for a while. After that I've no idea.'

She pulled in another lungful and exhaled slowly.

'Are you skint?'

'As a cow after a butcher is finished with it.'

She stubbed out the cigarette and stood up.

'Do you think Martin is in trouble?'

'I don't know. Were you and him an item?'

'None of your business.'

She reached for another cigarette. She had the habit bad or she was nervous. It was hard to tell which.

'We used to be. Not long after you turned up on the scene,' she said. 'At first he was just a good customer. In a way he probably paid for a fair chunk of this flat. Then things changed. I didn't want to charge and he didn't want to pay. He didn't seem to mind that other guys saw me and for a while things went along well. Then he upped sticks and moved south. Not a word. One day he was here - next, all I get is static. I didn't see him for the best part of ten years and then one day he rolls up at my door and wants to carry on as if he had never left.'

'When was this?'

'Four years ago. I told him that I wasn't interested. He wouldn't take no for an answer at first and even tried to pay me, but I held firm. He vanished again only to reappear the week before I came to see you.'

She stopped and went back to the cigarette. I waited for her to continue and risked sitting on the settee.

'He appeared again only this time he wasn't interested in me. He hands me a letter and says he needs it delivered to you. He puts a thousand pounds on the table and a scrap of paper with the prison name on it. So I do the good girl thing. After all a grand is a grand.'

A thousand pounds? It seemed a hell of a lot for a small errand.

'But you are back with him?' I said.

'You can't teach an old dog new tricks. He started pestering me again. Only this time he did it in nice way. He sent flowers. He called, but now he was as polite as I had ever known him to be. Then one night he turned up in a limo. Corny or what. He had two tickets to the Rod Stewart concert at Hampden. He knows I'm a massive fan and the tickets came with a meet and greet with Rod. How could I say no?

He was a changed man. After a great evening he kissed me on the cheek and left. A week later and we were back on again.'

'But he hasn't phoned since Tuesday.'

'Not a word.'

I looked at the clock and so did Rachel but she showed no sign of moving.

'Is your work far?'

'Thirty yards. I rep in a car. A Blue Mondeo. My first call isn't until ten and it's only a mile away. Fancy a cup of tea.'

I nodded and she vanished into the kitchen. I had no idea why the change in attitude. Like Maria's change of mind in Spain, women seemed a mystery to me at the moment.

I got up and went to the window. The morning was coming on strong and it looked like the sun was going to be a winner. I spotted Rachel's blue Mondeo and for a split second I saw a figure to the left of the car before he disappeared round the corner.

On gut feel I stepped back from the window, counted to thirty and stepped back again. The figure was there and, when I reappeared, he bolted. I recognised him and my heart froze. It was one of the goon patrol. How the hell did they find me here?

I did my party trick again and caught him out again. Not the brightest light-bulb in the box. Rachel came back in with two mugs of tea.

'I need to go,' I said.

'Fuck me. One minute I'm throwing you out and you hang around like a wet puppy. I make you a tea and you want to go. Where to - the hostel?'

'Rachel you don't need me in your life. I'm trouble and at the moment I'm more nonsense than I'm worth. I didn't mean for you to get mixed up in this. I just needed a bed for a night and your name popped into my head.'

'Get me mixed up in what. Are you telling me that there's more to you turning up than just looking for a bed?'

I dropped my head a little.

'You don't need to know.'

But she did. If the goon patrol really wanted me and I did a runner they might decide to use Rachel as a 'punch and tell' machine to find where I had gone.

'There are two men after me. At least I think there are two. There could be more.'

'And?'

'And one of them is standing at the corner of your street doing a crap job of pretending he's not there.'

She crossed to the window and looked out.

'Black jacket and blue shirt with greasy hair?'

'That's him.'

'You brought them to my house?'

'Not deliberately. I didn't know where I was going last night.'

'So they followed you.'

'No. I checked. I made sure I wasn't being followed before I told the taxi driver where I was going.'

I told her the story of last night and she laughed.

'And you didn't think that they might check with the local taxi firms for any pick ups?'

'It ain't that easy. They don't just hand out that sort of info to anyone. Plus I left from a strange address.'

'Big is it? Eaglesham? Do they have a lot of taxi pick ups at two o'clock on a Tuesday morning?'

'But they would need to have an 'in' with the firm.'

'Or they just lean on the controller. What would you rather do? Give out a fare's details or have your head caved in? Come on, you did it all the time in the old days.'

She could be right. She was probably right.

'So why not break in here and take care of me?'

'Maybe they only just found out where you are. Maybe they didn't want a witness. I don't know. Who are they?'

A good question. I really didn't want to go into the whole story but it looked like she was in this, one way or the other.

'You know the French man that Martin said I was in trouble with. Well I think they are working for him.'

'And is Frenchie bad news?'

'You have no idea.'

'Brilliant. So now I'm in the crap with you. If you fuck off do you think they are going to let me go freely about my business without answering a few questions?'

I shook my head.

'Genius. Fucking genius. I said you were bad news and I was right on the money. Shit.'

She stubbed out the cigarette, gulped the hot tea as if it was cold and lit another cigarette.

'This is not fucking good. Do you think they will risk coming in here?'

'Maybe. After all they had no qualms about breaking into Martin's house last night. For all they knew he could have been at home.'

Rachel sat down at the window table and looked out and said, 'He's still there.'

'We need to go. He's not that stupid that he doesn't know he's been spotted. I take it we can get out the rear and through the back green?'

'Sure and then what? You piss off and I wait for a knock. Good thinking, batman.'

'Well we can't stay here.'

'Why not? We wait on them, I hand you over and I'm home free. I would say that sounds about right for me.'

'Dream on. They're not going to lift me, or worse kill me, and let you hang around to ID them.

The French man is not stupid. Like it or lump it we are in this together for a while.'

'I'm not in anything with anyone.'

I said nothing and I saw resignation cross her face. I had seen that look on a hundred people's faces when they realised there was no way out.

'I have an idea,' I said 'I need time to sort this out. If I can square it with the French man then you are off the hook. I just need space to figure out how. Once I'm sorted then you are sorted.'

'And if they catch us? Then what?'

'You are no worse off than you are right now.'

She cracked another cigarette and stood up. I watched her pace around the room and wished she would just get on with making the only bloody decision that she had available.

She walked up to me.

'OK. We leave and then you sort out your shit. If you don't then I'm going to take things into my own hands. Agreed?'

'Agreed. Now let's get the fuck out of here.'

'We need my car. It's the only transport I have and we won't get far on the bus.'

She paced some more.

'I have an idea how to get to it without any violence'.

Rachel had hidden talents and, as she told me what to do, I smiled thinking that she would have made a fine addition to my team in the old days.

She rummaged in the kitchen and packed some stuff under her coat. We exited the house and made our way to the ground floor. Rachel opened the door to the back green and slipped out of sight. I made for the front close.

I emerged into a warm day. Nice day to die I thought.

The goon was standing at the corner and when he saw me he stiffened. I walked towards him, but kept to the other side of the road. Twenty yards along the pavement I stopped. He stared at me and then his mate joined him. I walked another few feet and then a few more. They started to cross the road and I stopped again.

When they were half way across I lifted my hand and, with a flourish, flicked them a V. They went into overdrive and sprinted to the pavement. I turned and showed them my heels. At Rachel's close I dived in and ran to the bottom of the stairs and stopped.

The goons barrelled in to the close and saw me. I put leather to concrete and headed out the door to the back green and they followed.

As I ran into the space behind the tenement I hung a sharp left and dropped to the ground. A clothes rope was lying next to the wall and I picked it up, hauling it towards me. With Rachel at the other end the rope was pulled tight about two feet off the ground.

The goon patrol hit the rope at full speed and my palm picked up a rope burn as the material was dragged through my hand. The men went down and Rachel was up and heading for the door. I joined her, but one of the goons was quick and reached out - grabbing my foot. I twisted but he held tight. I shouted out and Rachel turned to see what was going on.

The second goon was trying to get to his feet. Rachel ran back and, with a kick that Bruce Lee would have been proud to call his own, she landed her heel on the first goon's head. He screamed and let go of my foot. I pulled myself through the door and Rachel followed me. She slammed the door shut and turned the key that she had left in the lock. The sound of the second goon hitting the door reverberated around the close and we ran.

Outside Rachel hit the remote on the car key ring and we leapt in. She fired up the car and we were history.

'Now where?' she said.

'London.'

'What?'

'London. I need to sort this and the only place I can do that is London.'

'I can't go to London. I've got a job.'

'And it won't be much use if you're a new addition to Linn Crematorium. London it has to be.'

'Fuck.'

It's hard to think that you could spend six hours in a car with someone and say so little but Rachel was the type of girl that could do that and some.

We hit the outskirts of London just after rush hour and I directed her to Fulham. I had someone I needed to see and I could only hope they were still in their old house.

As we passed by the Albert Hall I had a change of mind and told Rachel we should check into a hotel for the night. I needed to do a little leg work before I took the next step.

We booked into one of the myriad of hotels that circle the Albert Hall. It took me back to that first night in London. This time I wasn't sharing. Separate rooms of course.

Another day another dollar.

Wednesday August 13th 2008

I've made a shed load of phone calls and I'm certain my name is now around town. But I had no choice. If there was one person that might know where Dupree was it was Giles - and the last time I had talked to Giles he had screamed at me down the phone for my little jaunt into Silvertown. Stepping on his toes had got him fired. But I knew he hadn't vanished.

While in prison I met a small time con called Casper Turner. Casper was a toe rag and had been caught robbing an old folks home. Normally I would have ignored his type but I recognised the name from London and I knew he had been tied up with Giles in some way. I caught up with him in the exercise yard and he told me that Giles had retired back to his house in Fulham.

When Giles got the bullet he was in his late fifties and I knew he had more than enough cash to get by. I thought he might be dead by now but the phone calls had revealed that he was very much alive, and still living in Fulham. I had an address and it was time to pay a visit.

Rachel was still in silent mode and when I asked to borrow her car it was like asking a kidney patient to lend their dialysis machine. But she agreed.

London was the usual - busy and a pain in the arse. I wound my way towards Giles's address. Harrods slipped by and then Stamford Bridge. There was a football game on tonight and the police cones were already going out to limit parking.

I turned into the North End Rd. The daily market was running, the stalls lining the full length of the road on my right. I had no sat nav and no A to Z but I knew Fulham well enough to get to Giles's street.

Parking was a different game and even mid morning it took me twenty minutes to find a space. Rachel's car was two inches longer than the gap but a bit of bumper to bumper action and I was in. I'd explain the scratches if she noticed them.

Giles lives in a row of terraced houses. In the mid eighties they had provided a surprisingly cheap accommodation option given their proximity to the city centre. Chelsea, just up the road, was already awash with million pound plus homes while you could still get a two bed flat for thirty five grand not half a mile away.

I walked past Giles's house and glanced at the building. The curtains were open but it was hard to tell if there was anyone home. I reached the bottom of the street and did a u-turn and gave one more fly by. I u-turned again and this time walked up to the door.

It was a jet black affair with a large brass knocker in the shape of a horse's head. I tried to remember if Giles had been a horse person, but there were no bells ringing. I pulled back the knocker and let it drop. I repeated the exercise and waited.

I was about to knock again when I heard a noise from behind the door. There was a spy-hole just above the horse's head and I saw it darken as someone looked out. Bolts were thrown and the door cracked open. A head appeared.

'Fuck.'

I seemed to have this effect on people at the moment.

'You can piss off.'

I smiled.

'What the hell do you want?' said Giles.

'To chat.'

'What the fuck do we have to chat about?'

'Amongst other things, the price of bread would seem a good topic.'

The door closed, a bolt was thrown and the door re-opened. Giles was dressed in a pair of battered chinos topped off by the granddaddy of oversized cardigans. The sort that has no buttons and relies on a cloth belt to keep it closed. He stepped back and gestured for me to come in. I took a quick look up and down the street but it was clear. I wasn't expecting anyone but then again I had thought Rachel's a safe bet.

'Expecting company?' said Giles.

I shook my head. 'Not unless you are?'

He closed the door, led me through a short hall and into the room on the right.

It was like stepping back in time. The furniture was Victoriana, as were the carpet and fittings. Two walls were floor to ceiling with books and the third wall had a stunning landscape of a ship in the midst of a hell of a storm.

'Take a seat. Tea?' he asked.

'Thanks,' I replied.

With that he left me and I wondered why there was no butler. I didn't sit down, choosing to browse the book-shelves instead.

I was no great reader but then again this was not Waterstone's top ten land. Most of the books sounded like medical texts from an era long since gone.

'The Establishment of the Causes and Effects of Excessive Bile and other Digestive Juices on the Well Being of the Elder Man', 'Vibratory and Motion Maladies', 'Searchlights on Health: Light on Dark Corners.' and so on. Rivetting. I moved to the second wall and it was more of the same. As I waited on Giles to return I hunted for a non-medical book but, if it there was one, I didn't find it before tea and biscuits appeared.

Giles placed a silver tray on the walnut coffee table that sat in front of two over stuffed armchairs. The tea was in a silver pot, the sugar in a silver bowl, the milk in a silver jug and the spoons were silver. The tea cups were delicate bone china. It could have all been cheap tack but, to my untrained eye, it all looked genuine antique.

Giles sat down and looked at me. I took the chair next to him but he made no attempt to pour the tea.

'Good tea needs to infuse for a full five minutes. My apologies for my brusque language at the door. I was caught a little unawares.'

The change of attitude was a bit too Jekyll and Hyde for my liking.

'So what can I do for you?'

'No small chat?'

'Do you want to?'

'No.'

'Then what can I do for you?'

'Do you know a French man called Carl Dupree.'

'Dupree. Wasn't he the one responsible for your little residency in prison?'

'That's him.'

'I can't say I know much. When you so kindly replaced me I decided to put all that behind me. I've heard of the man. A player as I recall. Big time down here. Other than that not a lot. Why?'

'I'm trying to find him?'

'For a social call?'

'You could say that.'

'And what makes you think I can help?'

'You were always well connected. Far better than me.'

'It didn't do me much good.'

'I mean well connected across the board. I never mixed in some of the circles you did. I was hoping that some of your old connections might be able to put me in touch.'

Giles leaned forward and gave the tea a stir. Clearly the five minutes were not yet up.

'Surely he can't be that hard to find? I mean he is hardly a low profile type of person.'

'No but my old network is long gone. I've probably exposed myself just getting your address. By the time I find him he will have found me. I thought you might be able to shorten the process.'

'If I could help why would I want to? After all you rolled me over big time. I don't owe you a thing.'

'Bygones are bygones?'

He laughed and stirred the tea again.

'Let's risk it.'

With this he poured milk into my cup and filled it with tea. He did the same for himself. I picked up the cup and took a sip.

'Well?' he said.

'Well what?'

'The tea. Was it worth the little wait?'

'Very nice.' And it was.

'I tell you what,' he said. 'I might be able to help but I want something in return.'

'What?'

'When I left, you took on my office. I never had the chance to clear it out.'

I remembered the office well. It wasn't quite in the same league as this room but you could see that he was on his way to a full blown life that revolved around Queen Victoria and her subjects.

'There was a globe of the world that sat next to the window. Do you remember it?'

I did. It was a huge beast.

'Do you know where it is?'

It was my turn to laugh. Of all the bizarre things to ask, I actually knew where the damn thing was.

I had stared at it for months after moving in and hated it. It was one of those globes that showed the world as they thought it looked in the late sixteenth century - missing chunks of land, odd shaped versions of countries, extra islands at the foot of the world - you know the sort of thing. Only it wasn't that old. Spencer used to say it was late Woolworths.

In time I had decided to clean out the office to put my own stamp on my space and the globe went.

I was all for throwing it out but Martin decided he wanted it. I had no idea he even liked the thing so I said yes and he took it.

'Martin Sketchmore took it.'

Giles couldn't have known Martin that well but his face changed markedly when I mentioned his name.

'You remember Martin?'

'Yes.'

'Well I can give you a number but he's gone a bit A.W.O.L. at the moment. It's the best I can do.'

'Maybe later,' he said and that seemed to close the conversation on the globe.

'So will you help?'

Giles poured another tea and offered me the same but I refused.

'There used to be a Sainsbury's at the end of my road. Did you know that?' he said.

'No' - a bit leftfield again.

'A small one. It closed. You don't hear of many supermarkets closing. It sat right at one end of the North End Rd market. It had a fruit and veg section but with the market outside the front door it never did well. It also had a hostel for Sainsbury employees above it. Young kids starting out were put up there until they got on their feet. All gone now. Funny how things move on isn't it?'

I didn't know what to say.

'You think you've got a handle on the world,' he continued. 'And then it sneaks behind your back and shoves you flat on your face. I loved that little Sainsbury's. I don't know why but when I found out it had the hostel I always thought of it as a nursery.

Lost souls in London being watched over. It had a nice ring to it.'

More tea was drunk and I waited for the trip down memory lane to resolve itself into a relevant story or vanish.

'Mid eighties it would have been,' he said. 'Mid eighties and I was walking home. I'd dropped the car in town after I had drunk too much and taken the tube to Fulham Broadway. The place was alive with football supporters. Chelsea were playing Millwall in the cup - at least that's the way I remember it.'

He sipped at his cup before continuing.

'The police had thrown a line of horses down the centre of the North End Rd keeping Chelsea fans to one side and Millwall to the other. It didn't really work - there was too much distance between the horses to make an effective barrier. A fan, I can't remember if it was Chelsea or a Millwall fan, thought it was funny to light up a newspaper, run up to one of the horses and try to set light to its tail. The policeman was off the horse in a shot and a scuffle broke out. A few more policemen on horses rode in and the fan was lifted. As I arrived at my road I looked up at the hostel above the supermarket. The lights were on and by now it was late. I saw a face at the window, looking down on the scene below, and I remember thinking that they don't really know what is going on down here. It's funny but some people can stare at a situation for years and never really get it. Strange that, isn't it?'

Leftfield. Definitely leftfield.

Giles finished his tea.

'I don't know where Dupree is but I can find out. It will take me a day or so. Give me a number and I'll let you know.'

'Can I call you instead?'

He shrugged his shoulders. 'Sure tomorrow night about seven should be fine. Where are you staying?'

'East end of the city,' I lied.

He gave me his number and the conversation was over. A few minutes later and I was back on the pavement.

I'd always thought Giles was a bit off the wall and old age hadn't really changed him for the better.

Back at the hotel I told Rachel we were here until at least tomorrow night and she kept up the silent treatment.

With nothing better to do I wandered up to the Natural History Museum and then across to the V & A and blew a few hours. I ate in a Pizza Hut. I don't know where Rachel ate. I had one drink in the bar and then called it quits for the night.

Thursday August 14th 2008

I woke up early but had nothing to do and all day to do it. I borrowed fifty quid from Rachel and decided to do the tourist bit. I waited until the rush hour had gone and picked up a Zone card that would give me travel all day.

I had no plan so I drifted through the centre of London seeing much but taking in little. My head played around the upcoming encounter with Dupree but the event seemed distant and unreal. I wasn't sure what I was going to do when I caught up with him, but doing anything was better than this nothing.

I walked up the stairs at Bank tube station and went for a wander around the financial city. You could almost feel the money in the buildings around me but you could also feel the tension. There was change in the wind. A few days ago the French bank BNP Paribas had signalled some serious financial problems and the issues over the summer with the US markets didn't bode well.

I wound my way up to Holborn and then walked along to Tottenham Court Rd. I cut through Leicester Square and took my time crossing Trafalgar Square before I made for Hyde Park and some green.

I found a bench and watched the lunch time people become the mid afternoon people. I got bored and stiff before deciding to go back to the hotel.

I grabbed a sandwich from a corner store. I wasn't hungry but I forced myself to eat it. God alone knows what might happen tonight and the last thing I needed was to be low on energy.

I lay on the hotel bed until six thirty and then headed back out. I found a phone box and, at bang on seven, I phoned Giles's number. It rang half a dozen times and then the answer machine kicked in. I was about to hang up when he picked up and apologised.

'I was in the toilet. Your French man has an office on Lloyds Avenue in the city. He operates his business under the company name King to Ace Ltd. I don't know the number on Lloyds Avenue but it isn't that long a road. I don't expect to hear from you again.'

Before I could say thanks he hung up on me. I didn't know Lloyds Avenue but there was a Food and Wine across the road from me and, after a quick transaction, I owned a shiny new A to Z.

The book told me that Lloyds Avenue was not a spit from where I had been earlier in the day. It backed onto Fenchurch St station and was a short walk from the Tower of London.

I went back to the hotel to find that Rachel was out. I scribbled a note and pushed it under the door. I didn't know whether Dupree would be at his office and I suspected a phone call at this time of night would prove fruitless.

I tried to look up the company in the hotel phone book but there was no entry under King to Ace. I borrowed the reception phone and tried directory enquiries but the people with the answer didn't have an answer. My best bet was to pay a visit and suss out the lay of the land.

I took the tube across town - still busy with late workers and night shoppers - before exiting at Bank. This afternoon I had turned left at the top of the exit - this time I turned right. The light was fading and the streets were quiet. Office lights were on all around me and the bulk of the city work force had split for the day.

I found Lloyds Avenue. It was short and unobtrusive. Not off the beaten path but certainly near the verge. I walked down the right hand side and scanned the few doors that there were. I completed the trip and repeated the walk, scanning the other side. I came up blank. I started again but this time I walked up to each door regardless of what the wall plaque, or sign outside, read.

About half way down there was a double door entrance. The reception area beyond was small and functional but the building had the feel of quality. The sign outside read 'Cranchester Aggregates plc'.

At the back of the reception, unmanned, was a list of the divisions and which floor they occupied. Most were a variation on Cranchester - Cranchester Equipment, Cranchester Haulage and so on. Right at the top, the style of sign writing changed.

All the bottom floors were written in simple capital letters - each in the same typeface. The top one differed in two ways. Firstly there was no letters and secondly there was a picture of the King of Hearts and the Ace of Clubs.

I pushed at the door and found it locked. There was a buzzer on the wall but I left it be. I placed my face up against the glass and squinted to get a better view of the sign but at this distance my eyes couldn't focus. Even so I was sure I had found the office. Now I just had to get in.

I stepped down the stairs and ducked out of sight from the reception. There was a CCTV in the lobby pointing at the door and I didn't need to advertise my presence anymore than I had to. I waited on the off chance that some one was working late.

I heard footsteps behind me and I ducked down, pretending to tie my shoe laces.

A pair of shapely legs glided by and turned up the stairs. I stood up and walked behind the owner of the legs. She took out a plastic fob and waved it below the buzzer; there was a click and she pushed the door open. I stepped forward and held it open for her. She stopped and looked at me.

'I'm looking for King to Ace? Is this the right building?'

'Top floor but you are supposed to use the buzzer.'

'Sorry I didn't know.'

'There's another buzzer on the reception desk. Donald is on night duty. If you press it he'll come. He might take a while but he will come - the buzzer is linked to his walkie talkie.'

'Can't I just go up and see them?' I said pointing at the sign on the top of the board.

'No. They have a key for their floor. Without it the lift won't go up that far.'

'Thanks.'

She walked to the lifts and I stopped at the reception. I waited while she got in and, as the doors closed, I walked towards the fire stairs at the rear of the lobby. I had no intention of calling Donald.

A quick look at the board confirmed King to Ace were on the seventh floor. I pushed open the door to the stairs and began to climb.

I was certain that the fire exit to the seventh floor would not open from the outside but with a bit of manipulation fire doors can be opened.

Six floors later and I was breathing heavily. I had met no one on the staircase and now a pair of fire doors lay between me and the next flight of stairs. It didn't look too legal to me. Why place a set of doors on the fire escape? To my left was the exit to the sixth floor. I opened it and looked in.

The whole floor was carpeted in thick wool - not cheap and not very practical. I suspected the sixth floor was the domain of the privileged few that ran Cranchester Aggregates plc.

Beside the lift doors there was a glass panel and glass door. Beyond this was a series of doors running off a corridor. The corridor was dark and there were no lights from the offices. I closed the door and turned my attention to the double doors that blocked my way to the next floor.

The fire doors had no handles and I suspected they had push bars on the other side to allow people out in an emergency. I tried to prise my fingers into the gap between the doors but they were tight to each other and a metal plate, that ran from floor to ceiling, covered the gap between the doors. The locking mechanism that sprang the doors when you pushed the bar was hidden from sight behind the metal plate.

I took out my tool kit and selected a small strip of metal that had a bend at right angles about two inches from the end. I slid the bent part behind the metal plate and ran it down until it met resistance. I left it hanging there and took out another strip of metal - this time with no bend - and inserted it below the bent piece of metal and pushed up until it stopped. Holding the straight piece steady I pulled down sharply on the bent strip and there was a click. I pulled at the door with the bent metal strip and it opened.

Grabbing the door I pocketed the two small jimmies and slipped through the gap, pulling the door behind me.

As expected the stairs continued up and, two flights later, I was faced with a gunmetal grey door. I turned the handle and the door gave. Beyond the door lay the lobby that serviced the solitary lift and beyond this there was another door.

This time the door was a solid wood affair polished to within an inch of its life. The wooden door sat in a large panelled frame and there was no way to tell if there were lights on beyond it.

I crossed the lobby and glanced at the numbers that sat above the lift door. Fortunately the letter G was lit. No one was on the way up.

Surprisingly the wooden door was unlocked and I pushed it open to find a narrow corridor that opened into a small vestibule. To the left of the vestibule sat a desk. Behind it two glass doors dominated the wall.

I entered the corridor and crossed to the desk. Apart from a phone and a computer terminal it was bare and I turned my attention to the doors.

The darkness suggested there was no life and my planned encounter with Dupree was looking like a busted flush. I tried the glass doors and they opened.

The lack of security spoke of confidence or stupidity or…

Light flooded around me and a hand from behind pushed me into the room. I went flying across the floor and fell to the ground. Before I could react someone dropped on me from on high and the wind rushed from my lungs. My arms were pulled behind my back and I was lifted up and pressed against the far wall. Hands searched me and pulled out the small knife I had hidden in my socks. My tool kit was extracted and both were tossed to one side. Next I was thrust sideways and down into a chair.

The attacker stayed behind me the whole time. Once in the chair he reached round my neck with his forearm, pulled back and my throat started to close up. I tried to struggle but the attacker was strong as an ox and held firm. I felt panic set in just before he eased off and I sucked like a good one. He paused for a second and then repeated the treatment.

A door at the other end of the room opened and one of the men from the photo in Inca walked in.

'The boss will see you shortly.'

With this he turned heel and left. My attacker eased off but kept a firm grip and there was little I could do but wait.

Ten minutes later the door opened again and the photo man appeared again.

'Bring him.'

The arm around my throat was removed and my left arm was pushed up my back - forcing me to stand up. The attacker frog marched me to the door and through.

The light in the room was dim and the atmosphere carried a faint scent of something sweet. The decor was lavish and some familiar objects littered the space. I spotted the globe that Giles had been on about and I wondered how it had got here. There was a painting on the wall of a man in full military parade uniform standing in front of a set of iron gates that guarded a large stately house in the distance.

To my left there was a long sleek marble table and at the end was a man sitting in a high-backed leather chair. The chair was turned away from me and I could hear the sounds of fingers on keys. The glow of a computer screen leaked from around the chair.

The attacker walked me to the other end of the marble table and sat me in the only other chair in the room.

'It's ok you can leave,' said the voice from behind the leather chair.

The men left - my mouth opening wide as the chair turned and the voice and the face came together.

'Martin?'

He smiled and pushed back in the chair.

'What the hell are you doing here? Where is Dupree?' I said.

He smiled again.

My head went into carnival mode as I tried to figure out what the hell was going on. Martin just kept grinning. Like the cat that got the cream AND the fish from the fish tank AND the bird that had always got away.

'What…'

I trailed off.

Martin sat forward.

'Drink?' he said.

I didn't respond but he still got up and pressed at a panel in the wall. A door popped open revealing a well stocked drinks cabinet. He poured two large measures of Ardbeg 18 year old into two odd shaped glasses.

He handed me one glass.

'The Glencairn Glass' he said, pointing to the glass in my hand. 'Odd that no-one ever thought to design a glass for whisky over the centuries. Brandy has its balloon, wine a goblet, sherry a sherry glass, champagne a flute but whisky never has had a glass designed to bring out the best in the liquid.

A small company in Scotland hit on the idea and created the glass in your hand. A small base to keep your hand away from the whisky - that stops you heating it up, it's made of crystal so you can hold it up in to the light and see the colour of the liquid and it has a tapered mouth to focus the aroma. Clever really - a bit odd looking but a smart piece of thinking.'

He returned to his seat and began sipping at the whisky.

I was still speechless.

'Not like you to be so quiet,' he said.

'Martin what the fuck is going on? Is this not Dupree's office?'

'In a manner of speaking.'

'So where is he?'

That stupid grin reappeared.

'Bloody stop that and tell me what's going on?'

'What do you think?'

'I don't know. Where is Dupree?'

'Have you ever seen Dupree?'

'Of course I have. Now where is he?'

'Have you ever talked to him?'

'Not as such.'

'Do you know much about him?'

'What is this? Twenty questions? Where is he?'

'Dead.'

'Sorry?'

'Dead.'

'When?'

'Fourteen years ago - give or take.'

'That's nonsense.'

'Cross my heart.'

The bastard couldn't be dead. He couldn't be dead for two good reasons.

Firstly he had been running the show since I was put in prison and secondly no bastard that I wanted that much dies on me before I could kill him. Christ, he had been keeping me in check since I got out. He had...

I looked at Martin and things became a little clearer.

'There never was a man called Carl Dupree,' I said.

The smile was back.

'Go on,' he said

I shuffled uneasily.

'There was never a Carl Dupree? Is that right?'

'Not quite, but you are on the right track.'

'You?'

A smile.

'You.' I said again. 'There is no Dupree and you are sitting here. You are sitting in Dupree's seat.'

'Keep going.'

'No Dupree. Then it was you…'

'Keep going.'

The bastard was going to split his cheeks if he grinned any harder.

'It was you all along?'

'Well done. Give the man a cigar.'

The floor seemed to slip and I had to grab the table to stop falling to the floor. Martin was behind it. Behind it all. I felt sick - deep down sick.

I stared at the table trying to get my thoughts in order.

'Why?' I stammered.

His smile widened. I didn't think it was possible, but he found a few more millimetres of curl in his lips.

'You figure it.'

I had a feeling that the last thing I wanted to do was figure it all out. I tried to unscramble my head and what emerged was not a sweet place in anyone's language.

'You ran the whole show?' I said. 'You did it all?'

'You could say that.'

'Shite!'

'You think so?'

'Martin I'm not into this game. Just fucking tell me what is going on?'

'Simple really.' He took another slug of whisky. 'Revenge really.'

'Revenge - for what?'

This time he laughed hard. Very hard.

'You don't know. You really don't know.'

'I have no idea what the fuck is going on. Revenge over who? Me?'

'Who else?'

'For what?'

'What do you think?'

I let go of the table and tried to get on board the train.

'For what I did in Glasgow with Read?'

'Well done.'

'What, twenty fucking years ago? You've done all this for something that happened two decades ago?'

'Of course. Why else?'

'For grassing you up to Read?'

'A hole in one my son.'

'But I brought you down to London. You did bloody well out of London.'

'So did you. Did you think I was just going to let you roll me over and do nothing? When you grassed me up, you shat on my life from a height you can't believe. I was completely shafted. I had to leave Glasgow. Leave everything I had behind. Every bloody thing. You had no idea how well I was doing. Our breaking and entering was just the start. I was on the verge of a hell of a deal and you dropped Read on me. He was a serious heavyweight and you set him on me like a dog on a bone'

'Jesus Martin. I stopped you robbing the bastard's house. Think what would have happened if I hadn't.'

'Bollocks. You turned turtle to save your own neck. You knew you were dead meat once he found out you had been in his house. I'm not fucking stupid. If I'd seen his name on the list from Rachel I would never have gone near it.'

He had stood up and his face was starting to match the deep red glow of the room.

'You have no clue as to what I had to promise to get back. It was easy for Rachel - she just waited a while and went back. But when I tried to go back it seems that I wasn't so easily forgiven and three of his morons took great pleasure in putting me into the Southern General for two weeks.'

'I'd been in London working my way up the ladder when I heard the wind was blowing a new way so I made a call to Read and promised him the earth if I could move back. With the sniff of a London gang coming north I reckoned whatever debt I owed Read would be buried with him when things changed - and I was right. When you rolled up at the front door again I saw my chance.'

'But you were my number two in Glasgow. I called you down to London and you came.'

'Like a lapdog. I might have hated your guts but the money was bloody good. When you said to go south, I knew I could swing it to my advantage. It was easy. You were losing it. You were starting to believe in your own hype - all that Riko crap. People were laughing at you behind your back. It was the easiest thing on the planet to convince everyone that you were becoming a liability. Once you took over the whole gaff you went off the deep end and people started to talk seriously about moving you on. The old man might have been a bastard but he was fair. You were acting like a tit.'

'So who was Dupree?'

'An out of work actor who owed me thirty grand and had a drug habit to support. Good wasn't he? Me and Spencer simply sat in the background and pulled the strings.'

My head was getting sore with this.

'Spencer as well? Shit. So why didn't you just off me and have done with it?'

He began to pace the room.

'I wasn't going to let you off that easy. No fucking way. I wanted to see you suffer. I so wanted to see you suffer. And I also wanted what you had. So when you pulled me down to London after topping the old man, Spencer and I went into overdrive. We set you up like a turkey at Christmas. You played along like a gem. You went nuts over the Dupree stuff. You became obsessed. We couldn't have dreamed you'd be so stupid. All we had to do was dump anything that had our name on it and then hand over everything else to the police.'

'You told me that you had no choice in the witness box.'

'I didn't. I needed to do it to make sure you went down. By then you were so hated that I thought someone might take you out. Prison saved you. I had a few guys on the inside watch your back for the first few years.'

'Look after me? I took a kicking every second day at the start.'

'And you would have been on the morgue slab after a week if my guys hadn't stepped in.'

'Fourteen years Martin. Fourteen fucking years.'

'Not long enough. If it was down to me you would have rotted in there.'

'What happened with Spencer?'

'Got greedy so I sent him home. He really did die in a car crash near Oban.'

I tried to stay in front of it all, but my head was boiling up a stormer of a headache.

'What the hell was all that Stevie, the key and Spain stuff. What in the fuck was all that about?'

He sat back down again and took a sip of whisky.

'I couldn't resist. You made it so easy. When I knew you were getting out I sent in Rachel with the letter. I thought you were getting out sooner than you did but I got it wrong. It didn't matter - you were like a rat down a drainpipe once you started on the trail. I laid down the breadcrumbs and like a bird you followed along.'

'The code, the safety deposit boxes. What about Mallorca Security?'

'Mallorca Security is part owned by me and Ryder. It was easy to set it all up. Maria was in on it from the outset.'

'You're wrong. If she was then why did she hit the alarm and save me from your goons?'

'Stupid cow panicked. It was meant to end there and then. I'd had enough fun and wanted you back home. I thought the whole photo and code thing a laugh but enough was enough, and people were beginning to look at me in the same way they looked at you when you obsessed on Dupree. At least I recognised the signs of obsession. It was more than you did with Dupree. By the way you did well getting out of Mallorca. How did you do it?'

I ignored him.

'Charlie Wiggs?'

'Charlie owes me big time. I've kept him on as my accountant since our days. He's into me for an arm and a leg and it wasn't hard for me to get him to play along. '

'Charlie's friend in Mallorca?'

'Ryder's son or rather his stepson. How else do you think he would have got a copy of the blueprints so easily?'

'So why let me get this close to you?'

'I had no choice. You slipped my guys in Spain. You did it again at my house. I was in London trying to sort out the mess in Mallorca at the time. I still thought you were on the island. When you didn't turn up on the return flight I figured you must have got home somehow so I sent some muscle to my house with orders to pick you up if you were there. You did well. Very well. But I knew you wanted to front up to Dupree. So I waited for you to reappear and reappear you did. I had lost you right up until you phoned Giles.'

'He is in it as well?'

My voice rose a shade.

'Of course. Once you skipped on us at Rachel's house I figured you would come after Dupree so I put the word out to all the old gang that there was cash in it for anyone that let me know where you were. When Giles phoned I set up our little meeting. You know that all you had to do was press the downstairs buzzer. The cloak and dagger stuff was a little OTT.'

I had a million other questions.

'So everything - prison, the warnings, Mallorca - the whole fucking lot was for your amusement?'

His grin was back big style.

'Absolutely. And tonight is the money shot. I needed to see your face when you realised who had been behind it all. This is my special moment.'

A silence blew into the room and he downed the last of the whisky in his glass. His grin vanished and I could see his eyes glaze over.

'But somehow it's all a bit hollow. I don't know what I expected but it wasn't this. I thought I would feel vindicated but I don't. I feel, well sort of empty.'

His grin had been replaced with a small grimace and a weary look crossed his face.

'This feels all wrong.'

Damn right it felt wrong. I stood up fast and was half way across the table when the door burst open and I was grabbed mid air before being thrown to the floor.

'All wrong,' he said. 'All wrong.'

He walked up to me as the attacker picked me up and slammed me back into the chair.

'Did Giles tell you his stupid Sainsbury's story. The one to do with the Chelsea/Millwall game? Did he?'

I said nothing and the attacker wrapped his arm around my throat.

'He's told me it on more than one occasion. I always thought it a bit of a crap tale. I mean what is it supposed to mean, but you know what? I think I might know what that face looking out the window was thinking. I think that face belonged to someone that knew exactly what was going on but chose to stay in the safety of the hostel. He wasn't a little innocent. That face had been, seen, done and bought the t-shirt and knew he was in the right place that night. Well you're in the wrong place. I'm sorry old friend that it has to end like this. I need to get on with life and that's not going to happen with you around.'

I tried to say something but the attacker flipped me from the chair and suddenly my mouth was full of carpet. Martin bent down.

'If you wanted Dupree this badly then you'll want me with sugar on. I can't have that. So I'll say my goodbyes.'

The bastard kissed the tips of his fingers, reached down and patted me on the head. I looked up and saw the smile leave his face.

'So different. It should have all been so different.'

I struggled to get up but my attacker and the man from the Spanish photo were good for the game and I was pinned to the floor. The first fist caught me behind the ear - the knuckleduster slicing open my skull. Snap, crackle and pop and the second fist mashed my nose to mince.

Just the beginning. I tried to curl into a ball. Just the beginning.

The door to the room closed as the bastard left and it was time for more pain. The attacker reached between my legs and grabbed at my balls. The squeeze was so hard it felt like one of them burst. A thumb searched for my left eye socket and a forefinger for my right - fluid spurted and darkness fell.

Then they got serious.

Chapter 21

Hi I'm back. Are you still there? Of course you are. Was the diary interesting? I bet it was. Giles has done a wonderful job. Hasn't he?

Sorry it finished in August. As you may have gathered things didn't go well after my meeting with Martin. Not well at all. In fact it is a miracle I'm still here. Four months in hospital on account of the beating I took.

I've lost the sight in both eyes. The doctors have told me I'll be blind for life. Both my legs are useless. One of the kicks - or maybe it was a couple of the kicks in Martin's office broke my back and severed my spinal chord. I'll never walk. I can't even piss on my own. My left lung will never work again and the damage to my kidneys means I will need a transplant, but I'll not be high on the priority list. My pancreas is shot and my liver isn't much better. The doc says that he is amazed I'm still here.

I can't use either of my arms. A stroke took care of that a couple of months ago.

Sorry I had to duck out there but everyday at twelve o'clock they take me away for a little physiotherapy. Not that it does much good but I'm hardly in a fit state to refuse.

I don't get many visitors. Rachel came by with my stuff a while back but she said little. Giles Taylor showed up and he has been a good friend in these last few months.

He was a wonder with the digital recordings. His patience was startling. You can't believe how much nonsense was stored away on that little recorder's memory. He interrogated me like a good one, to add meat to the bones, and I had him read it all back to me when he was finished.

I think he should get the damn thing published.

Giles was the first new face in a while and now you are here.

But you're not a new face.

Are you?

Martin Sketchmore would be closer to the mark.

Wouldn't it?

Surprised? Thought a little silent treatment would fool me?

Oh I know who you are Mr Sketchmore. I may not be able to see you but I don't need to. I set up your little visit. I take it you got the note - Giles again - about the diary. About the fact that I had put everything I knew in it. Why else would you be here?

Oh I know you are supposed to be from the psychiatrist. A listener - that's what he called you. A listener. People who are happy to listen to people like me. No hopers. But you're not, are you? You're Martin. I can smell the aftershave. You still like Boss.

Well I hope it was worth it? The diary that is. It is what it is but it's hardly going to be your downfall now is it? I mean what would someone do with it if I had passed it on? Is there anything in there that would cause you much grief? Not really. Anyway I'll be dead soon and you can have the thing - for what it's worth. So no worries there then.

I bet you were surprised as fuck to hear I had made it out of your office alive. Must have come as a shock to find out I was still breathing.

Your boys left me for dead. They dumped me in a rubbish skip at the back of the Lloyds insurance building. Like yesterday's rubbish. I'm sure they thought I was dead and I wasn't far from it. The bin men found me in the morning. It took a fourteen hour operation to save me. That and six more operations and I'm still worth shit.

Now look at me. What good am I to man or beast? I'm sure there are people out there who are in a worse state then me and wake up every morning thanking their God that they are alive - but not me. I can't live like this. I've been lying here for weeks and all I can think of is what you did to me. How you ripped away my life. Played me like a fiddle and then tried to have me killed.

I wish you had succeeded.

You talk about revenge and how you obsessed. Wasn't that your word? Obsessed over me. Well Martin I've obsessed over you. Far more than I obsessed over Dupree. Must be in my nature.

I've done more obsessing in the last few weeks than you would think possible. I've spent every waking minute thinking of ways to get back at you.

Remember Giles's story about the boy in the window looking down on the street. Well I don't think he did know what was going on. Not really. Deep down he was missing the big picture. You see what was going on down in the street wasn't really anything to do with him. He wasn't part of it. He was just a bystander. Watching. Not understanding.

A bit like you at the moment.

You're a bit of a bystander. A watcher. Not a listener. No, if you were a real listener you might have picked up a few clues along the way. A few hints that gave away that I knew who you were.

But you didn't listen. Not really. And that will cost you.

It was Giles who gave me the idea. You might not know this but Giles hates you. Not as much as I do, but he hates you all the same. He's told me all about the errands and humiliation you have put him through since he retired.

It seems that I underestimated you. I always knew you had an evil streak but Giles is an old man who only wants a quiet life and you keep dragging him back into a world he long ago thought he had seen the last of.

So we got chatting, Giles and I, and, as I said, it was his idea. Well at least in part. It wasn't the cleverest of ideas. It doesn't have to be. Getting you here was the easy bit. The next bit is a little tougher.

I'm sure you've heard of an I.E.D. They're on the news all the time. Improvised Explosive Devices. All the rage in Iraq and Afghanistan.

I suppose you also know that we are in a private wing of the hospital. The rooms either side are empty. Have been for a few days. There are new people due in tomorrow but I think they may have to find other accommodation.

When Giles first came up with the idea, I was supposed to come back from my physio session and find that someone had blown the crap out of my room. You would be in the middle of it. The casualty of a bizarre crime. Pay back complete.

That was Giles's idea. But I couldn't leave it at that. I needed to know you had read the diary. I needed you to know what I have gone through. I needed you to have every little detail of my life in your head. After all, you were the one who said you obsessed on me. You must have a serious obsession to sit through my life story in silence, to read the diary and even now to sit there and say nothing.

I also had a moment when I was recounting my life story. How high had I flown? How much did I have? And now what? That's when I decided to change the plan. After all we have been through a lot together so why not say goodbye together?

I'm sure you know what is coming next and you can run if you want to, but you won't make the door. I may have lost my eyesight but my hearing still works and I can hear your breathing.

Hard and fast.

See this silver handle here. The one with the red trigger on it. I know it's red - I had Giles describe every inch of it. The one that is peeking out from under my pillow. Well when I drop my head on it there is four pounds of plastic explosive under my bed that will go up. It's on your side if you would like to look. Giles set it all up last night. I've sweated all morning that it would be found but it would seem that, for once, my luck is in. They didn't even spot it when I went to physio.

And you are still here. I thought you might have done a runner but true to type you needed to hear how it all panned out. You just couldn't pick up the diary and go. After all what harm can a quadriplegic blind man do?

I'm sure there are questions. I know I have many but, sadly when I got back into bed, I bounced my head on the trigger and the device has a two minute delay.

If you run you might just make it.

But I doubt it.

The End

Also by Gordon Brown

Falling

Prologue.

The door to the toilet slams open and I turn to the noise. Two men in suits, one tall, one small, barrel across the tiles and pin me to the wall. The tall one is grinning like a cat on speed and he grabs my arm, spins me around to connect with the fist of the short one and I go into stun mode.

They are strong and the tall one kicks my feet from under me and they haul me out of the toilet and onto the fire escape. I try to resist and receive a slap to the head for every word I utter. Seven slaps - I'm a slow learner.

We hit the roof at full speed and I'm lifted clean off my feet and hurled over the edge.

Once by Gordon Brown.(Coming soon)
<u>Chapter 1</u>

The sun is in the sky and the clouds scud by. My heart is racing and all is right with the world.

And cows piss gold.

Another day dawns and the curse of work calls. The alarm is lying against the bedroom door. It isn't broken, but a few more mornings of abuse and it will be time to order another one from the internet - if I can afford it. I know I'm going to be late and I can't afford the luxury. The world is going to hell in a basket as far as my employer is concerned. The world is always going to hell in a basket as far as my employer is concerned.

The room has a smell of damp that I'm usually immune to but last night the rain came down with no intention of stopping until the clouds were wrung dry – and then some. When I got in last night the leak in the roof over the toilet had easily filled the bucket that I kept there for just such weather.

I've given in asking Mr List, my landlord, to have it fixed. My lateness with the rent has a direct correlation with the repairs on the flat and I am very behind on the rent.

The rainwater had flooded the toilet by the time I got to bed and it is only a matter of time before Charles comes up from the flat below to complain. Not that it will make any odds. He rents from Mr List as well.

In a fit of unusual generosity I took it upon myself to try and plug the leak earlier in the year.

Since then the leak has been worse by a factor of five.

I can smell the hall carpet as the residual heat in the building tries to dry the sodden material. At least it has stopped raining.

I need to get up and add to the damp. The shower no longer has a curtain. I pulled it down when trying to get out of the bath two months ago. If the rain water hasn't encouraged Charles to climb the stairs then the shower water will.

I pull the covers back and gasp at the cold. Even in a t-shirt, y fronts, an old pair of jogging bottoms and a scraggy cardigan there is little I can do to stop the heat loss. I had the electric fire on last night for an hour and that probably means I need to feed the machine before I can make a cup of tea.

Shower over, I head for the kitchen. My premonition was right and I'm out of electric credit. The cold shower was testament to this. I need a cup of tea but the animal in the hall only takes one pound coins and I have exactly thirty two pence in my pocket.

I drink a glass of water and scrape out the remains of a packet of Cornflakes and chew them dry. The clock on the wall tells me I'm on time to be late. I can't afford to be late. I grab my jacket and hit the stairwell at speed. Charles is on his way up and I tell him that I've reported it to Mr List. And he tells me that isn't good enough. I'm out of shouting range and through the front door before he can get into a real one.

The sun really is shining a little today because the bus queue is still there and if the queue is still there then I haven't missed my bus. I root around for my monthly pass and thank someone else's God that the company provide me with it as part of my wages. If it was down to me I would be walking every day.

The bus is the usual mix of condensing breath and stale clothes. In both cases I am a major contributor. I am too late to get a seat but at least I'm on the thing. The woman next to me is using me as a bumper on all left hand corners and the man on the other side on the right hand ones. She has an air of drink about her. Last night's. Lucky cow.

The bus pulls up at my stop and I get off and head across the road to the nineteen sixties concrete shell that I call work.

I reach for my work pass and swear. It's sitting on my bedside cabinet. I approach security and they look at me as if I just fell from the sole of someone's shoe. Temporary pass in hand I enter the inner sanctum of the factory through the electronic gates and my day has started.

My boss catches me as I arrives and gets sarky over me being on time. He tells me I'm on the factory floor today. Rubbish duty.

I drop down two floors and pick up a stylish white boiler suit that doesn't fit. I push through the plastic slats that keep the hot air inside the factory and enter a world of noise.

Around me the plant is a dinosaur. A relic of the seventies and eighties when people outnumbered robots. Our factory makes plasters. The sort you put on your cut finger. They make them the old fashioned way. Rows of women - and it is all women - sitting at machines that look like cinema projectors only, instead of reels of film, there are reels of material that are mashed together to make your every day plaster.

A woman shouts my name and I wave back. She points to the rubbish bin that sits in front of her station and I realise that she isn't being polite but wants it emptied.

The girls start an hour before I do and when you are on rubbish duty they all want emptied first.

I spend the first hour lifting bins, traipsing across to the recycle point and emptying them. I know this game well. If I'm quick and smart I can get ahead of the game. Not by much but by enough to grab a quick break. If I'm too slow the bins are never empty and I can spend from now until tea time hauling them.

The rubbish I collect comes from the paper covers the giant rolls are wrapped in. The women aren't allowed to stop the machines to empty the bins and that is where I come in. At least that is where I come in today.

I don't mind this job. Compared to some of the others in the factory this is an ok gig The women are chatty, the rubbish is clean and we get three breaks a day and when the horn goes at four thirty there is already a queue of people waiting to swipe out.

What I couldn't know was that Mary Sadler was going to be killed by Jean Laidlaw.

To be fair neither did Mary Sadler but then again it wouldn't matter much to her in half an hour.

<u>Books published by Fledgling Press</u>

Stella Maris, by Nan O'Dell (2001)

Bag Lady, by Nan O'Dell (2001)

Gertrude, by Brian Fine (2002)

Defending the realm, by Brian Fine (2002)

Four score, by Ilsley Ingram (2002)

Soldier of the queen, by Malcolm Archibald (2003)

Horseman of the veldt, by Malcolm Archibald (2005)

Selkirk of the Fethan, by Malcolm Archibald (2005)

Aspects of the Boer War, by Malcolm Archibald (2005)

Everyman's Worst Nightmare, by Stacey John (2006)

Mother Law, by Malcolm Archibald (2006)

The New Fledgling Cook Book, by Bridget Wedderburn (2006)

Inner Thoughts, by Christine Tindall (2007)

Powerstone, by Malcolm Archibald (2008)

Granpaw's Cook Book by Bridget Wedderburn (2009)

Falling, by Gordon Brown (2009)

59 Minutes, by Gordon Brown (2010)

Tenterfield: My happy childhood in care, by Margaret Irvine (2010)

Forthcoming (2010):

The Sinkable Wife, by Jock Stubble.

All available from any good bookshop, or direct from www.fledgling.co.uk.

Some free excerpts downloadable from www.weefreebooks.co.uk